Too
COOL
FOR this
School

BOOKS BY KRISTEN TRACY

FOR TWEENS
Bessica Lefter Bites Back
The Reinvention of Bessica Lefter
Too Cool for This School

FOR TEENS
Crimes of the Sarahs
Death of a Kleptomaniac
A Field Guide to Heartbreakers
Lost It
Sharks & Boys

FOR KIDS
Camille McPhee Fell Under the Bus

Too COOL FOR this School

Kristen Tracy

DELACORTE PRESS

This is a work of fiction. Names, characters, places, and incidents either are the product of the author's imagination or are used fictitiously. Any resemblance to actual persons, living or dead, events, or locales is entirely coincidental.

Text copyright © 2013 by Kristen Tracy
Jacket art copyright © 2013 by Linzie Hunter

All rights reserved. Published in the United States by Delacorte Press, an imprint of Random House Children's Books, a division of Random House, Inc., New York.

Delacorte Press is a registered trademark and the colophon is a trademark of Random House, Inc.

randomhouse.com/kids
Educators and librarians, for a variety of teaching tools, visit us at
RHTeachersLibrarians.com

Library of Congress Cataloging-in-Publication Data
Tracy, Kristen.
Too cool for this school / Kristen Tracy. — First edition.
pages cm
Summary: Twelve-year-old Lane Cisco has good friends, a secret boyfriend, and the position of sixth-grade captain at Rio Chama Middle School, but life gets complicated when her off-beat cousin Angelina arrives for an extended visit.
ISBN 978-0-385-74070-8 (hardback) — ISBN 978-0-375-98962-9 (glb) — ISBN 978-0-375-89984-3 (ebook)
[1. Middle schools—Fiction. 2. Schools—Fiction. 3. Family life—Fiction. 4. Friendship—Fiction. 5. Cousins—Fiction. 6. Conduct of life—Fiction.]
I. Title.
PZ7.T68295Too 2013
[Fic]—dc23
2013011084

The text of this book is set in 12-point Baskerville MT.
Book design by Vikki Sheatsley

Printed in the United States of America
10 9 8 7 6 5 4 3 2 1

First Edition

Random House Children's Books supports the First Amendment and celebrates the right to read.

For Wendy Loggia:
You are brilliant.
And my characters benefit
because of it.

• 1 •

The eighth graders got to choose us. That was how the system worked. Leslie Fuentes and Robin Galindo stood before us in all their eighth-grade glory looking super fashionable and super powerful and super serious. And I understood why. Who they chose mattered. Because Leslie and Robin would be stuck with their picks for the entire school year.

"You know your speech is going to be recorded?" Robin asked, holding up a small camera in one hand and a tripod in the other.

I did not know this.

"Do you guys mind waiting here while we set up the equipment?" Leslie asked.

I knew the correct answer to that question, so I said, "I don't mind."

It caught me off guard when somebody had a better answer. A cute seventh-grade boy stood up. "Do you need any help?" He was the only boy here.

"We've got it, Derek," Leslie said, slinging a stylish canvas bag over her shoulder. I noticed that her bag's lavender stripes matched the lavender pattern on her sandal straps. She must have bought them together. Or maybe she was the kind of person who hunted for matching lavender patterns all the time. I wondered what her bedspread and pillows looked like. I suspected they were very lavender-y.

"Well, I'm great with electronics if you change your mind," Derek said.

I stopped looking at Leslie and turned my attention to Derek. His follow-up offer reeked of strategy. I mean, did he always brag about how great he was with electronics? Was he *really* such a helpful person? Or was it all an act? I suspected the latter. The longer I stared at Derek, the less cute he became. In fact, he was *way* less cute than my secret boyfriend, Todd Romero. It didn't even matter that Derek was a little older than Todd. Derek had hang-ups.

I mean, why did he use so much hair gel? His dark curls looked wet and crisp at the same time. Sort of like plastic. Why would you want to have a plastic-y head in middle school? Todd had normal hair that looked great, especially when he played soccer and the wind blew it.

Once I realized that I'd been staring directly at Derek's head for at least two minutes, I quickly looked away. Before I decided to try out for class captain, I had no idea

I had this much paranoia and nervousness and judgment inside me.

Shortly after Robin disappeared into the gym, she burst back through the door into the hallway. "We accidentally drained our battery. It'll be a couple more minutes."

"I can help with that!" Derek cheered.

He was so eager.

"We've got it, Derek," Robin said.

Robin left me and my competition sitting in a semi-circle of metal folding chairs while she bouncily reentered the gym. The fluorescent light flickered above us, making the hallway feel grim. My mind wandered. Did I really want my speech recorded? Did that mean it was going to be watched again and again? I hadn't really designed my speech for repeated viewings. Sure, it was well crafted and sincere. But when I'd written it, I'd assumed it would only be heard once.

As you probably already know, my name is Lane Cisco and I'm running for sixth-grade class captain because I am very capable of keeping myself and those around me highly organized. I am assertive and flexible and very open to other people's thoughts and suggestions. I promise to come up with innovative ideas to help make this year very fun for everybody.

I closed my eyes and kept focusing on my speech. Was I forgetting something? I thought I might be. Then I felt a small bump against my shoulder.

"You look like you're zoning out," said the girl next to me.

I opened my eyes. That seemed like a rude thing to tell a person after you bumped her. "I am not zoning out," I said. Then I stopped talking. Because I realized that this comment came from a very small fifth grader. And I didn't have time to converse with a fifth grader.

I mean, I didn't even know any of the fifth graders' names. That wasn't useful information. The fifth graders didn't matter. Neither did the seventh graders. Every grade got their own class captain. Except for the almighty eighth graders, who historically had gotten two. Coral Carter and Paulette Feeley, two of my fellow sixth graders, were my only competition. I glanced down the semicircle of chairs in their direction. They were dressed to impress. Paulette, who traditionally arrived to school zipped into a dumpy denim jacket decorated with sea horses, had actually worn a gray corduroy skirt and soft pink tights. It was an alarming and stylish turn of events.

If it were just a lottery, I wouldn't have been so nervous. My speech wouldn't have mattered and neither would my outfit. My fate would have been determined by a slip of paper or the flip of a coin. Either I'd win or I'd lose. It would be so simple.

"Do we have a faculty mentor?" the fifth grader asked. "Is she in the gym?"

A bunch of us looked toward the gym. The class captains had had a faculty mentor last year: Ms. Knapp. Where was she? It did seem a little weird that the eighth graders were running the show.

"I plan to ask as few questions as possible," Derek said.

That seemed smart.

The door flew open again. "Let's start with the fifth graders," Leslie said. Her face looked so serious; her perfectly glossed, lavender-tinted lips never even turned toward a smile.

The fifth graders plodded into the gymnasium in one frightened and fashion-challenged clump. All three of them were wearing tacky tinfoil bracelets. Those things had been popular at camp, but nobody in my crowd was lame enough to think you could actually wear jewelry made out of aluminum foil to school. That fashion statement belonged back in the woods, where all my friends and I had left it.

"Good luck," Derek said.

Wow. He was so fake. Was it wrong to want somebody I vaguely recognized and had officially met less than ten minutes ago to lose?

Once the gym door slammed shut, it was impossible to hear anything. What took place on the other side of that door was one of the biggest mysteries at Rio Chama Middle School. Nobody ever talked about it. Not the winners. Not the losers. All we knew was that decisions were final. And those who were chosen became part of an elite group of students who had special power. In addition to attending monthly pizza meetings with faculty members and offering student input, class captains got to plan the three school parties: Halloween Carnival, Winter Festival, and Spring Movie Night. Plus, as a bonus, a framed group photo of the captains was hung in the school's central trophy case.

And that picture didn't get taken down and thrown away once the year was over. It got moved to a pillar, where it would remain forever. Me. Smiling. Class captain. Forever. I wanted that. I really, really did.

The gymnasium door burst open again. *Slam!* And the small fifth grader, the one who'd bumped me, came running out like she was being chased by a pack of killers.

"Did you win?" Derek asked.

But she didn't stick around to answer. Then, before we had a chance to talk about her, another girl raced out of the gym. And she looked weird. Like she was covered in glitter.

"Maybe *she* won," I said. "Do they glitter bomb you if you win?"

A seventh-grade girl frowned and smoothed her long brown hair. "I hope not. Do you know how hard it is to shampoo glitter out of your hair?"

I did not. My hair was medium long and brown and not terribly thick. I had a tough time making it stay in a ponytail. Plus, I hadn't used glitter since kindergarten.

"Neither of them won," Paulette Feeley said with complete certainty.

We all turned to look at her. How could she possibly know that?

Coral looked surprised but offered her own explanation. "I guess their faces did look really freaked out."

Coral was right. And I made a mental note that whether I won or lost, I would not let my face look too freaked out.

Leslie appeared at the door. "We're ready for the sixth graders."

My whole body felt hot and uncertain. "What happened to the other fifth grader?" I asked as I shuffled along behind Paulette and Coral. It was as if the third girl had been vaporized.

"I'm pretty sure winners exit out the back," Paulette said.

Paulette seemed to know a lot about how this top-secret process worked.

I wasn't the only person who noticed this. The energy surrounding the competition shifted from excitement to high-stakes tension the minute we entered the gymnasium. As soon as the door clicked closed, Leslie and Robin spun around and began scrutinizing us with their eyes.

"This has never happened before," Leslie said, pointing a purply-polished fingertip at Coral.

Robin took one step toward us and angrily waved her hand, which was a gesture I wasn't used to seeing because I came from a mellow home.

"I am stunned and appalled!" Robin snapped, waving her hand more erratically.

"There's a squealer on the loose," Leslie blurted out as she rummaged through her bag.

I stood beside my competition and pressed my lips together, trying to look as concerned as possible.

"Get the blindfolds!" Robin said, her voice tinged with urgency. "We're getting to the bottom of this right now."

· 2 ·

It was rare for me to find myself in a situation that required a blindfold. But once we stepped onto the basketball court, things went from tense to weird with lightning speed.

"This is a *major* crisis," Robin said.

It was enormously disappointing news to hear, because I wasn't built for crisis. I wished my friends Ava, Lucia, and Rachel were here. They knew how to manage drama much better than I did. Robin handed me a dark piece of oval fabric with a rubber band stapled to it.

"Put this on," she demanded.

I didn't argue. After I slid the blindfold over my eyes and nose, I couldn't see anything. Even light.

"Who said that winners exit out the back?" Leslie asked.

I did not say a word. I even tried to keep my exhalations silent. It was really too bad Ms. Knapp wasn't around. Because I doubted a faculty mentor would allow students to endure this sort of trauma blindfolded in a gym. Seriously. Our district had banned dodge ball two years ago, and we weren't allowed to touch each other with more than a finger when we played tag.

"Being a class captain is an esteemed tradition. We're looking for somebody with integrity," Robin said.

"Yeah," Leslie said. "Secret-sharers, spoiler-spreaders, and loose-lipped squealer-dealers need not apply."

I was certain that I wasn't any of those, especially not a loose-lipped squealer-dealer. I was a kind sixth grader. All my friends thought so.

"Nothing will happen until we start getting answers," Leslie said.

Standing inside my own darkness made me feel claustrophobic. Somebody needed to start giving answers.

Silence.

Somehow all the blackness made me feel as if the gymnasium's walls were falling in on me. How much longer could I take this? Maybe five minutes. But did I need to take it for five more minutes? That was when I saw my chance to get a little bit ahead in this competition. I mean, why drag this out and punish myself?

"Paulette Feeley told us that winners exit out the back," I said.

I heard three separate gasps. But wasn't honesty

supposed to be the best policy? Weren't we going to get to the truth eventually? Plus, the blindfold was starting to make the sides of my nose sweat, and didn't that cause pimples?

"How did you know that?" Robin asked. "Who squealed?"

That was a great question.

"It's okay. If you tell us the truth right now, nothing will happen to you," Robin said.

I really wished I wasn't wearing that blindfold. Because I was dying to see the look on Paulette Feeley's face. Dying.

"Yeah. Everything will be totally cool," Leslie said in a low voice.

When I heard somebody breathing in a spastic and nervous way, I knew it was Paulette. This was so much *drama*. Ava and Lucia and Rachel were going to die when I told them about it.

"By the way," Leslie said. "Everything that's happening right now is secret information."

This news was a huge bummer.

"We can't even mention the blindfolds?" Coral asked.

I thought that was a great question for Coral to ask, because it made her look like a person who *really* wanted to be a secret-sharer.

"Absolutely not," Leslie said.

"Tell us what we want to know," Robin insisted.

Silence.

"Was it Maya?" Leslie asked in a soft, kind voice.

All the pieces were coming together. Paulette's sister, Maya, had tried out for class captain last year and lost.

"Maybe," Paulette said.

"All we want is the truth," Leslie cooed. "That's the foundation of this organization."

And then Paulette spoke the four words that changed the course of everything.

"Yes," she said. "Maya told me."

"Oh," Robin said with a ton of disappointment in her voice. "That's too bad. I really liked her."

"Yeah, she was totally, totally great," Leslie said.

I found it spooky that they kept referring to Maya in the past tense.

"Okay," Robin said. "You'll need to leave, because from this point forward you're absolutely ineligible. And so is your entire bloodline."

"What?" Paulette asked. "My bloodline?"

"All your relatives. That's a bloodline," Robin explained.

"For how long?" Paulette asked. "A year?"

"Basically forever," Leslie said.

I heard somebody start releasing a terrible whine and I knew it was Paulette.

"Ouch," Robin said. "That hurts my ears."

Paulette immediately stopped making that awful sound. "Should I just leave right now?" she asked.

"No," Robin said. "We'll send the other loser out with you. Hold tight for three minutes. And keep your blindfolds on."

"Lane Cisco," Leslie said. "Follow us."

Did this mean I was the other loser?

"Do I keep the blindfold on?" I asked.

"Yes," Robin and Leslie said in unison.

"Okay," I said. I swung my arms out in front of me, trying to feel for them in the dark. But I didn't need to do that for very long, because their arms grabbed me.

They led me almost one hundred steps before we stopped.

"Sit down," Leslie commanded.

I reached behind me for a chair and when I felt the metal seat, I quickly lowered myself into it.

"Take off your blindfold," Robin said.

I did.

"You are underneath a disco ball," Leslie said.

I looked up and watched the rainbow-colored lights swirl across the room.

"Why?" I asked.

"It's top-secret and nobody knows it yet, but this is going to be the year of disco," Robin said, pointing at the ball and then shimmying her hips.

"Totally," Leslie said. "It's retro and cool."

"Um, yeah," I said, even though I barely knew anything about disco.

"Just standing here underneath it," Robin said, gesturing to the spinning ball, "makes me feel so much better about this whole disaster."

"Maya is so gross," Leslie said. "What's wrong with her?"

I saw my chance to gain a little more ground. "She's a spoiler-squealer," I said, messing up the phrasing a little.

Robin leaned over and whispered something in Leslie's ear. Then they both smiled at me.

"You're exactly who we want," Robin said.

Whoa. Did this mean I didn't have to give my speech?

"Really?" I asked. Ava and Lucia and Rachel had led me to believe that the competition for class captain would be brutal. Maybe even bloody. And Todd had said, based on an Internet rumor he'd read, that I needed to brace myself for something excruciating, possibly a competitive eating contest involving waffles. But this had been easy. I basically had just had to show up and behave like myself and they'd picked me. And it just kept getting better. Because they started giving me compliments.

"Let's face it," Leslie said. "You're totally class captain material."

"Yeah," Robin said. "You dress cute. You're smart. You're mellow. And you're friends with that girl who plays the cello."

"Cellos are so cool," Leslie said.

"Um, they really are," I said. It seemed a little weird that Ava's cello-playing abilities scored me additional points, but whatever.

"Do you have any questions?" Leslie asked.

Did I? Should I? In my mind, this wasn't how I thought things would happen. I felt caught off guard that they'd even expect me to have questions. Hmmm. "So you don't want to hear any of my speech?" That seemed like a solid question. I'd put so much work into memorizing it that it seemed like a total waste not to be able to use any of it.

"We only make people give their speeches if we're un-decided," Leslie said.

Robin blinked as if maybe I'd offended her. "We just told you that you're class captain. We're totally decided."

What was I doing? I'd won. Forget my speech. Forget asking solid questions. Why wasn't I acting totally thrilled? And that was when I exploded in excitement. I jumped into the air and yelled, "Oh my gosh! Thank you!"

"Group hug!" Robin cheered as she opened up her arms wide. The disco lights swirled across her body.

I didn't give my speech a second thought. Winning felt great. And so did getting complimented and hugged by two popular eighth graders. As we finally released one another from our group hug, I knew that sixth grade was going to be a mind-blowing experience.

"Don't forget to exit out the back," Leslie said.

"Absolutely," I said.

"And don't tell anybody about our theme yet," Robin said. "Not even your cello friend."

"I won't!" I promised.

I left the gymnasium that Friday certain of one thing: My life felt perfect. I didn't want a single thing to change.

· 3 ·

In addition to being mellow, my parents were also highly supportive. So after finding out that I'd won class captain, they offered to host a special dinner in my honor and let me invite my friends.

"Time for toasts," my mother said, lifting a goblet filled with sparkling apple juice. "Cheers to Lane."

I loved it when my mother broke out the Bohemian glass goblets. She and my dad had bought them together on a trip to Prague before they got married. The cut glass and colored stems looked impressive and made the night feel extra special.

"May your class-captain duties not detract from your homework and may your job remain forever stress free," my dad said.

I sort of wanted to complain about his toast, because it wasn't entirely cheerful. But I didn't. I knew why my dad had said what he said. He was stressed out about his own job, coordinating a groundskeeping crew at a local college. But being class captain wasn't going to be like managing gardeners on a college campus. I didn't have *duties*. I just got out of class early once a month to hang out with cool people and plan school parties. It was the opposite of stress.

"To sixth grade," Ava said. "And all the awesome things that are about to happen."

Even though it wasn't exactly to me, I thought that was a pretty good toast.

"*Mabuhay!*" Lucia said, lifting up her goblet.

Ava wrinkled her face in disapproval. "What does that even mean?"

"It's a Filipino toast. It means 'long life,'" Lucia explained.

Ava rolled her eyes. Just because she was a musician didn't mean that she automatically cared about cultural stuff like Filipino toasts.

"What a drag to start worrying about death right now," Ava said. "We're twelve."

"Not all of us," my dad said. "Some of us are approaching midlife."

"Rachel," my mother interrupted. "Do *you* have a toast?"

My mom was great at switching topics and smoothing over unpleasant moments.

"I do," Rachel said, raising her crystal goblet and clearing her throat. "Let's never forget our friends."

Rachel was the best.

Clink! Clink! Clink! Clink! Clink!

After dinner, in my room, we tried to cram in as much gossiping as possible, because even though it was a Friday, my mom wasn't letting my friends stay over.

"Paulette is such a mopey freak. What's wrong with her?" Ava asked. "Ooh! I think you should wear this." She pulled out a knee-length denim skirt from my closet.

"I like the buttons," Rachel said. She wasn't very interested in bashing Paulette or fashion planning. Rachel was my kindest friend. And every day she wore the same thing: T-shirt, jeans, and platform sneakers. Instead of combing through my closet with Lucia and Ava, she sat at my desk doodling marine life. Rachel was great at sketching squids.

"Don't you hate wearing skirts?" Lucia asked.

"Yeah," I said. But I thought I should dress up for my first class-captain meeting. Next week, in addition to discussing our (strictly confidential) disco theme, we were going to get our group photo taken. So if a skirt made me look better in the photo, I didn't mind wearing one.

"What about these?" Lucia asked, removing a cute pair of yellow jeans from my closet.

Ava shielded her eyes and fell to the floor. "I'm going blind!"

"They aren't that bright," I said.

"I like them," Rachel said, looking up from her latest squid. "They remind me of egg yolks."

Lucia put them back in my closet.

"Maybe I need to go shopping," I said. "Maybe I could buy something lavender at the mall to coordinate with Leslie."

"Gross," Ava said. "Don't do that. The mall sucks right now. All those extra security guards. If you're not twenty, they follow you around like you're already a felon."

"She's right," Lucia said. "After that last skateboarding incident, they're totally profiling tweens."

"Tuma ruins everything," Ava said.

Before I had a chance to agree with Ava about Tuma or defend the mall, my phone buzzed. It was a text from Todd! Ava knew that I had a secret boyfriend, but I didn't want to share the news with Lucia and Rachel until I was sure my relationship was totally solid.

"Who is that?" Lucia asked.

I read his text.

Todd: Are you around tonight? Want to talk?

This was exciting. I really wanted to send my friends home right away so I could call Todd. We didn't really talk that much on the phone. I mean, everybody knew we liked each other. We just weren't ready to be official.

"Is it something about class captain?" Rachel asked. "Is it something you can't talk about?"

My friends had been really awesome about helping me keep my class-captain things confidential by not asking me questions they knew I couldn't answer.

"Is it Todd?" Lucia asked.

She was so direct. And I didn't want to lie. I could feel myself blush.

"It was," Lucia said. "What did he say?"

For some reason this question made me feel very shy. My phone buzzed again. I looked and saw that he'd sent me a photo.

"He sent me a picture," I said.

"Of what?" Rachel squealed, sounding way too excited. She stopped scribbling squids and raced to my side.

I showed them the picture of Todd's dog, Ruby.

"Cute husky," Lucia said.

"It's a malamute," I corrected.

"Does it shed?" Rachel asked.

"It's a fur bomb," I said.

"Too bad," Ava said.

"Does Jagger have a dog?" Lucia asked.

Touché! I liked how Lucia was brave enough to fling Ava's own crush right in her face.

"Absolutely not," Ava said. "Mrs. Evenson is allergic to everything."

Ava's crush on Jagger Evenson wasn't nearly as far along as my relationship with Todd. But she was very hopeful. And with good reason. If those two could get it together, they'd make a great couple. They were both so cool. Plus, they were the same height.

"We need to figure out a way to make them eat lunch with us," Ava said.

"Who?" Rachel asked.

Rachel might have been kind, but sometimes she missed the boat.

"Todd and Jagger," Ava said. "They eat with the other guys, but I want them to eat at our table."

It bummed me out that we weren't focused on picking out my class-captain outfit anymore. But when we started talking about guys, it usually took all our focus.

"I don't think you'll be able to pull them away from the guy table until they finish playing that video game," Lucia said.

For weeks Todd and Jagger and a bunch of other guys had been trying to win a game involving two tribes of dwarves: *Dwarf Massacre 3: Axe of Doom*. I didn't really understand all the rules.

"That game is so lame," Ava said.

"Do you even know what it's about?" Lucia asked.

Ava dropped my skirt on the floor and sat down next to it. "You've got good dwarves and bad dwarves. The good ones are made of steel and the bad ones are made of iron. They're battling each other for world supremacy."

I was super surprised that Ava knew the rules to *Dwarf Massacre 3*.

"Maybe we should try to play it," Rachel said. "And then maybe we could hang out at their table and talk about our progress."

Ava groaned and collapsed backward very dramatically. "I'm strapped to my cello five days a week trying to learn my part for the waltz in Tchaikovsky's *Sleeping Beauty*. If I add one more thing to my life, I'll die."

"I'm pretty busy too," Lucia said. "I've still got five weeks left of Tagalog classes with my mom."

I was still surprised that Lucia agreed to take a conversational foreign language class with her mom. It seemed like a terrible way to spend your Thursday nights.

"Haven't you quit that yet?" Ava asked.

Lucia shook her head. "I've learned a bunch of practical phrases. I mean, I already know how to tell time."

"But are you ever going to visit the Philippines?" Rachel asked.

"Sure," Lucia said. "Someday."

"Let's try to keep brainstorming on how to get the guys to eat with us," Ava said.

We all just sat in silence. There was a strong divide in the lunchroom. Girls ate with girls. Guys ate with guys. It was hard to cross those boundaries.

"What would happen if we just sat with them?" Rachel asked.

Ava's eyes grew wide, but she didn't object.

"I'd try that," Lucia said.

But I thought sitting with my secret boyfriend before we agreed to be official might look pushy. "If you guys do that," I said, "I'm going to sit with the other class captains."

All of my friends gasped.

"No!" Rachel said.

"I'd miss you too much," Lucia said.

"You won't let being class captain change you?" Ava asked. "Will you?"

What a weird question. "Of course not," I said.

Then my phone buzzed again. It was another text from Todd.

Todd: Going to play dwarves with Jagger. Maybe we can talk tomorrow.

Oh no. I'd lost my chance to talk to him.

"Why do you look so sad?" Rachel asked. "What did he say?"

I shrugged. "He's going to play *Dwarf Massacre*."

Rachel looked at me very sympathetically. "Maybe you and I could learn how to play."

Did I want to pretend I was a dwarf who violently killed other dwarves? I didn't think so.

Knock. Knock. Knock.

My mom popped her head in my room. "Time to break this party up. Moms are here."

We all scrambled to our feet. Ava handed me my skirt. "You should totally wear this. You've got great tights."

"Yeah," I said.

They left my room and my house and soon I was all by myself. I washed my face and brushed my teeth and put on my pajamas and got in bed. *Does Todd want to hear from me?* I wondered. *Probably!* Even though I knew he was busy, I sent him a text.

Me: Are you winning?

I held my phone and stared at it. But nothing happened. Eventually, I set it on my bedside table. I pulled out a magazine and tried to do some reading. But my phone was very distracting. Then it finally buzzed.

Rachel: Thanks for dinner. Night!

I felt bad that I was so disappointed. Because Rachel was a great friend. I should have been happy to hear from her. I texted her back.

Me: Welcome! Night.

And while I continued to wait for Todd to text me back, my dad knocked on my door. "It's great that you've got such good friends," he said, walking in.

I lifted up my head from my pillow and looked at him. "Yeah," I agreed.

"But family is important too," he said.

I nodded. "I know. You and Mom are great."

"Right," he said. "And even though you don't see them every day, it doesn't mean you shouldn't care about your relatives. You know, your extended family."

My mom raced into my bedroom like she was missing something important.

"What are you talking about?" she asked.

"Extended family," I offered.

"Michael," my mother said in a stern voice. "Lane looks ready for bed."

I watched as my mother practically dragged my father out of my room.

"Not yet," she told him in a hushed voice.

And I probably should have wondered about that comment all night long, but I didn't. Because my phone buzzed.

Todd: Iron dwarves are kicking my butt.

I was so thrilled. Because not only had Todd texted me, but I mostly understood what his text meant.

Me: Isn't steel stronger?
Todd: Not in this cave.
Me: Good luck.
Todd: Ditto!!

I stared at that word for a long time. Ditto. With not one, but two exclamation points. I felt so lucky. I was twelve and I had everything.

· 4 ·

While becoming class captain changed a lot of things for me, one thing it did not change was my class schedule. I still had Mr. Guzman as my main teacher for English Language Arts, Social Science 6, Geography, and Creative Writing. And Ms. Fritz still taught Science 6, Algebra Readiness, and PE 6. But the great thing about Rio Chama Middle School was that even though I had two teachers, I didn't have to change classrooms. My teachers did. So my desk was my desk and I didn't have to share it with anyone.

This was a great arrangement, because I used my desk as a well-organized storage area. It was the kind of desk with a lid that lifted up, so I kept all sorts of things in it: lip gloss, magazines, notebooks, pens, exciting notes passed to me by my friends, et cetera. My desk was situated in the ideal place for sending and receiving notes. It sat kitty-corner from Todd, Lucia, and Jagger. So we had a good note-passing flow. I could pass any slip of paper to any one of my friends anywhere in the room. And because we were careful note-passers, we never got caught. And since Ava was just one row away, I was usually partnered with her for group work. It was a dream seating chart.

The day of my first class-captain meeting, I obsessed about what would happen. I knew we met for forty-five minutes in the administrative meeting room next to the secretary. But I had no clue what happened beyond that. Did they serve snacks? Who was going to be our faculty mentor? Would we take the group photo at the beginning? At the end? Would we start planning the Halloween Carnival? Ooh. Would we start purchasing carnival supplies online? I really hoped we'd start party planning as soon as possible. Because the more we planned, the better the party.

"You look really happy," Lucia said as she walked past my desk to turn in her Algebra worksheet.

I glanced up from my worksheet and smiled. I'd decided to wear my denim skirt with magenta tights and a white cotton top. Lots of people had given me compliments. Even Coral Carter, who I wasn't really interested in talking to and was actually trying to avoid. Beating people in a competition and then seeing them in class was awkward.

"Time to turn in your worksheets," Ms. Fritz said as she erased the white board.

Ms. Fritz was such a down-to-earth teacher. She wore jeans and chewed gum and flat-ironed her curly blond hair.

I thought that style made her look a little bit like a model. I watched as she walked down the rows collecting the last of our worksheets. When she got to my desk, she smiled and paused.

"Have I mentioned yet how impressed I am that you're our class captain?" she said. "I bet you'll bring inspiring ideas to our next pizza meeting."

It blew my mind that I was going to eat pizza with my teachers and possibly bring inspiring ideas. I mean, today I wasn't going to do that. Today was just a meeting of the class captains for orientation with our faculty mentor. And our group photo. But when it came time for our first pizza meeting, I was going to be beyond ready.

As soon as Ms. Fritz reached the back of the room, a note landed on my desk. I caught a glimpse of Todd's hand pulling away. I loved his notes. I had saved all twenty-seven of them all in a special compartment in my desk.

Why is your mom at school?

What? I turned around in my seat and looked at him. My mom was at school? I mouthed the word, *Where?* Todd made a scribble motion with his hand. He wanted me to write him back.

Where did you see my mom?

I released a fake sneeze and tossed the note onto his desk. He read it and wrote back in less than ten seconds.

In the attendance office.

Why would my mom be there? Maybe Todd was wrong. Maybe my mom looked like another person's mom. That had to be what it was.

"Lane," Ms. Fritz said, "We're going to leave for the gym now. You should head off to your meeting."

The fact that I got to ditch PE was pretty sweet. Because I wasn't the kind of person who was born with a strong desire to run back and forth and do push-ups while wearing our official school colors: yellow and black. Ooh. Maybe that was something I could tackle as class captain. Maybe I could make PE less lame by letting us wear non-school colors.

As I left my classroom, I realized that I was a little stressed out. Various worries tumbled through my brain. Where would I stand in the group photo? Should I sit? Kneel? I really didn't want to end up next to Derek. How did that guy even win? I thought the other winners would be like me. I guess Robin and Leslie looked beyond his plastic hair and saw something in Derek that I didn't. Worry. Worry. Worry. I needed to learn the fifth grader's name. But it wasn't urgent. Because, really, why were fifth graders even in middle school? It was weird.

When I got to the meeting room, there was a big paper sign taped to the door that said WELCOME, CLASS CAPTAINS. I walked through the door and noticed an entire table set up with cookies and crackers and punch and churros.

"Grab whatever you want and take a seat," Leslie said.

"Thanks." I picked up a paper plate and loaded it with sweets.

"We're all here now," Robin said. "There is some paperwork involved with your captainship. Derek and Fiona are reading over the honor pledge. You have to agree to follow the six tenets of honor and sign it."

"Okay," I said. I didn't have a problem agreeing to be honorable.

I took the honor pledge and my plate and sat down next to Derek, because that was the only empty seat at the table. I noticed Ava's cello case leaning against the back wall. On days when she had practice after school, the principal had given her permission to store her cello in the meeting room. I was always impressed that Ava could carry her own cello. Housed in a canvas bag, that instrument was almost as tall as she was.

HONOR PLEDGE

I will not lie.
I will not steal.
I will not cheat.
I will not tolerate unkindness.
I will guard and respect the traditions I am inheriting.
I will take ownership of my choices and do my very
     best.

That sounded reasonable. I signed it as quickly as I could and handed it to Leslie so I could start eating my cookies.

"Perfect," she said as she placed it in my folder, and blinked her bright eyes at me. She applied her lavender shadow in such a way that her eyes looked surprised and happy all the time. I wondered if she'd show me how to do that.

"Lane," Robin said, frowning at me from across the table. "Do you have to leave early?"

I shook my head. "No."

"I was just wondering, because I saw your mom in the office," Robin said. Then she took a big bite of her churro.

Why did people think my mom was in the office? Whose mom looked like my mom?

"Before the photo, I have an awesome announcement," Leslie said, leaning forward in her chair. "Ms. Knapp has agreed to be our faculty mentor again."

"That's great," Derek said. "She's so laid-back."

"Exactly," Robin said. "She agrees to everything."

"So let's start by reiterating our theme," Leslie said. She hopped out of her chair and raced to the white board. She wrote the word *disco* in big loopy letters.

"And let's also reiterate our class-captain nondisclosure policy," Robin said, joining her at the board. "Don't tell a freaking soul."

"When do we announce?" Derek asked.

"Next month," Robin said. "We'll need to make posters for the big reveal and put them up all over school."

"How many posters?" asked the fifth grader.

"A million," Robin said. "We'll blanket this place." Then she burst out laughing.

It was obvious that she loved being a captain.

"We should also mention our budget." Leslie said. "Before we announce, we'll want to price fog machines, disco balls, and DJs."

"Our budget is tiny this year," Robin said with a sour face. "But we consider these items essential for executing a successful disco party. It's gonna reek of ambiance."

"And we might be able to purchase a used fog machine. And that could be cheaper than renting one for all three parties," Derek said.

Robin didn't look thrilled. "We don't want to buy heavy equipment. Renting is easier."

I liked how she put Derek right in his place. Why did he think we needed to *buy* a fog machine?

"Any other suggestions?" Robin asked.

I couldn't think of one. And apparently neither could anyone else.

"Let's move on to the photo," Leslie said. "I brought lipstick in case you need to borrow some. You should always wear more makeup for photos than you wear in regular life."

"The flash dims your natural coloring, Fiona," Robin said, handing a colorful tube to the fifth grader.

"Definitely not my color," Derek said, passing the tube to me.

"You are so witty," Leslie said, blinking several times at Derek.

No way. Was Leslie flirting with Derek? Did Leslie *like* Derek? Was that why he won? It really wasn't fair that I couldn't share this information with my friends. Because Ava loved a good crush story. Derek set the tube down in front of me but I didn't pick it up. Wouldn't that makeup have other people's lip germs on it? Wasn't that how you spread mono?

"Let's get going," Leslie said. "Photos take place out front next to the cholla cactus garden."

"I hope I don't get pricked," Derek said.

Leslie laughed like Derek was the funniest guy she'd ever encountered in a meeting room. It was nuts.

I left the germy lipstick on the table and followed everybody into the hallway. And that was when I saw her. My mom.

At first she tried to pretend she hadn't seen me. She lifted a folder up, blocking her face from my view. But I'd already seen her, so that didn't work.

"Let's follow our photographer," Robin said, pointing to a guy with a white goatee wearing a cowboy hat.

That guy was standing almost next to my mom. My surprise quickly turned to panic when I realized that the only reason my mother would be at my school was if something was terribly wrong. So I forgot about following the goatee guy and I raced up to her.

"What's happened?" I asked. My mind spun and spun. Oh no! There had to have been a terrible tragedy. Was it a death in the family? All four of my grandparents were no longer alive. So it wasn't about them. I gasped. "What happened to Dad?"

My mother could see that I was beyond alarmed, so she pulled me to her side. "Everything is fine."

"But why are you here?" I asked. Moms didn't just show up to school when everything was fine.

"Congratulations!" the secretary said as she passed me. "It's always wonderful when family moves to town."

I had no idea what she was talking about. "Mom?" I said.

"Lane," Robin called. "We need to line up for the photo."

"I'm coming," I said. But I wasn't going to come until my mother told me what was going on. The only relatives I had lived in Alaska. Aunt Betina and her daughter, Angelina. Her father, Uncle Dave, had divorced Aunt Betina several years ago and was working in Toronto. My dad called him a deadbeat.

"Your cousin, Angelina, is coming to town," said my mother very cautiously.

"Really?" I said. "I thought Aunt Betina loved Alaska. I never thought she'd move."

"Lane!" Robin called.

"Aunt Betina isn't moving," my mom said very quietly.

That didn't really make any sense. How could Angelina move and not Aunt Betina?

And then my mother did something surprising. She called out to Robin. "Lane will be there in a minute. I need her help in the bathroom."

Why would my mother yell anything about a bathroom

while inside my school? I wanted to die. Instead of dying, I hurried behind her to figure out what was going on.

"This isn't how I wanted to tell you," my mother said, standing beside the paper-towel dispenser.

"Tell me what?" I said kind of rudely. "I can't be late for the photo."

"Listen, I want you to know that sometimes in life you find yourself doing something that lacks honesty," she said. "And you do this thing not because you want to be dishonest, but because there is no other way."

"I don't understand what you're telling me," I said.

"I'll give you the truncated version," she said. "Aunt Betina finally decided to marry Clark. And they've decided to honeymoon for a month. Her child care fell through. Angelina is coming to live with us."

Honeymoon for a month? Child care fell through? What kind of terrible mother was Aunt Betina?

"Stop making that face," my mother said. "This will be a once-in-a-lifetime chance for you and your cousin to bond. It will be good for everyone."

"Uh, I don't know about that, Mom," I said. We didn't have a spare bedroom, so I tried to imagine where Angelina would sleep. *My room?* There was only one sixth-grade class at my school, so that meant she'd be in *my class.* Would she eat lunch with me too? Would she expect to hang out with all my friends? For how long?

"I was hoping for a more positive reaction," my mom said.

"How long will she stay?" I asked.

"A month," my mom explained. "I told you her child care fell through."

"A month!" I stared at my mom like she was crazy.

"It's the perfect amount of time for two people to bond."

I'd only met my cousin a couple of times at family reunions, and we hadn't really *bonded* during those times. I tried to remember what she looked like and how she behaved, but I couldn't.

"The school district wouldn't allow a visitor to come for a month. So I had to change Angelina's permanent address to ours. That's why I'm here."

"Really?" I asked. That seemed illegal. "When is she coming?"

"Friday," my mother said.

"Friday!" I yelled. That was way sooner than I expected.

The bathroom door creaked open. It was Robin. "Hey, I'm sorry, but we really need Lane out front. We're paying the photographer by the hour. Plus, he needs to get to a dog show."

"Okay," I said.

I turned to leave, but my mother put her hand on my shoulder and stopped me.

"I think it would be best if you didn't tell anybody about this," she said. "We're fudging the rules a little bit."

I flipped back around so quickly that I banged into my mother's bulging purse. "I just signed an honor pledge five minutes ago."

She took a deep breath and rubbed my back. "I don't

want you to lie. Just don't discuss our situation with any-one."

First I couldn't discuss anything related to being class captain or having a disco theme. Now I couldn't discuss anything about my inbound Alaskan cousin. I felt a little bit burdened by all this secrecy.

"Go, go, go," my mother said, pushing me toward the door.

"I want to talk more about this when I get home," I said, sounding way too much like a parent.

"Absolutely," my mother said.

I hurried outside and found everybody standing in a line in front of a bunch of prickly cacti.

"Finally. Why don't you kneel in front?" Leslie said.

I liked the idea of being front and center, even if that meant I had to kneel in a dirt patch while wearing tights. When the photographer told us to smile and say the word "burrito," I buried all my worries inside of me, gave him a big grin, and said, "Burrito."

No, I wasn't happy about how my mother had handled this situation, but I guess sometimes things happen in a way that we didn't mean for them to happen. And we do our best and just move forward. Right? It was only for a month.

"Are you okay down there?" Derek asked as the photog-rapher moved his tripod closer.

"I'm okay," I said. I didn't know why Derek annoyed me so much.

And then, right as the photographer clicked the last

photo, I felt a flicking sensation on the back of my head. I flipped around to see Derek's finger curled in a position to flick me again.

"Sorry," he said. "I couldn't resist."

I was stunned. Derek shouldn't be flicking my head during our group photo.

"Don't flick me," I snapped at him. "I don't like it."

He smiled. "Okay," he said. "It will never happen again."

And I hoped that was true. The last thing I needed on top of all my problems was to be harassed by a fellow class captain. No. He needed to keep his flicks to himself. My life was complicated enough.

· 5 ·

Later that night, during our family meeting, my mother agreed that it was way too weird for me not to mention Angelina's visit to my friends.

"She can't just appear out of nowhere," I said. "I've got to prepare my friends for her. Ava has a difficult time adjusting to new people."

My dad laughed at this. He felt Ava was spoiled. But we all had our hang-ups, and I didn't have time to get into that with him. Basically, the way we left things at the family meeting was that I was allowed to tell my friends that Angelina was staying with us while her mother and new husband got things ready for their move.

"Don't think of it as a lie," my mom said. "Because you never know. Aunt Betina and Clark may decide to move here."

My dad shook his head. "Your sister will never leave Alaska."

And so that was how it was handled. That was what I was allowed to say.

I should probably have done a better job preparing my own life for Angelina's arrival. I should probably have emailed her or texted her or returned her single phone call to me. But even after listening to her message four times, I didn't quite know what to say.

ANGELINA: Hi, Lane! Your mom gave me your number. This is so great! I am super excited to see you again. At the last family reunion I remember that you had a toy horse named Buttermilk. Are you still really into horses? I like animals too. I mean, I LOVE the outdoors. Okay. I'm rambling. Call me back if you have time! Your mom says you're really busy. She says that you just won class sergeant. So cool! We don't have those in Alaska. Congratulations! See you Friday.

Class sergeant? I think Angelina's message was a tipping point for me. On Friday, when my parents were ready to pick her up at the airport, I just couldn't make myself join them.

"Are you sure you don't want to come?" my mom asked as she tied her jacket belt around her waist.

I wrinkled my nose and shook my head. "I'd better not. I'm behind with some important stuff."

"I think it's fine if she wants to hold down the fort. We'll be back in thirty minutes," my dad said.

"Maybe we should get a sitter," my mom fretted.

"I'll be fine," I said.

My mother finally agreed. "Okay. But try to do something productive."

Sometimes my parents treated me as if I was nine.

"I'm working on my creative writing homework," I said, lifting up my spiral notebook. "Mr. Guzman told us to write a poem from the point of view of one of our chairs."

"Really? I hope you say kind things about my butt," my father joked, shaking his rear end back and forth.

"Gross," I said.

My dad laughed again. "What a weird assignment. Can you believe that, Claire? Her teacher wants her to pretend she's a couch."

"A chair!" I called after them right as they slammed the door.

I decided it made sense to write the poem from the point of view of our wingback chair, which sat closest to the door. That was where most of our guests liked to sit. Of all the chairs in our house, it had the most severe butt dent. I'd only made it as far as the title, "Confessions of a Wingback Chair," when my phone rang. I didn't recognize the number. So of course I was hoping it was Todd calling me from a random phone. I wanted to let it ring four times so I didn't look too eager, but I couldn't stop myself from picking it up on the second ring.

ME: Hi.

LESLIE: I'm so glad you answered. It's Leslie.

ME: Cool. Hi, Leslie. I didn't recognize your number.

LESLIE: Haven't you programmed my number into your phone yet? You should really program all the class captains into your phone. Do you need me to email you those? I don't have time to do that now. I mean, I'm in a wicked hurry.

ME: Um, emailing them later works.

LESLIE: So what are you doing?

ME: I'm at home. Writing a poem.

LESLIE: Awesome. You are so deep. So do you have a pen?

ME: Yeah.

LESLIE: Okay. Write this down. You need to make two dozen cookies for our cookie basket for Ms. Knapp. We like to look grateful, especially at the beginning of the year. Robin is making peanut butter. Derek is making magic bars. Fiona is making lemon squares. And I'm making chocolate chip. We need a fifth kind.

ME: Wow. Ten dozen cookies for Ms. Knapp?

LESLIE: Teachers like to share. Moving on. Robin thinks the basket should have a vegan option. Do you know a killer vegan recipe?

Ring. Ring. Ring.

LESLIE: Is that your doorbell? Do you have to go?

ME: No.

It was the first time a class captain had called me. It seemed like I should stay on the phone until *she* had to go. *Ring. Ring. Ring.*

LESLIE: Don't worry about putting them on a cool-looking plate. We'll arrange them in the basket using special cookie sleeves. Robin's mom is a florist. She has an eye for that stuff.

Ring. Ring. Ring.

LESLIE: Do your parents hate answering the door or something?

ME: They're gone.

LESLIE: Wow. You're lucky. My parents didn't leave me home alone on weekends until this year.

ME: It's not like they do it all the time.

Ring. Ring. Ring.

LESLIE: I'm so torn right now. I totally have to go. But I think I should stay on the phone with you. Until you answer the door. Because what if it's a psycho person?

ME: It's probably just FedEx.

LESLIE: Not this late. Are you expecting anybody?

Do you read the police crime log online? There's been a ton of break-ins on the west side of town. Don't you live on the west side? I probably shouldn't be talking about those.

I took a deep breath and began walking toward the door. I didn't even know the police kept a crime log. I mean, I rarely ever thought about crime. Unfortunately, I did live on the west side.

Ring. Ring. Ring.

LESLIE: So creepy! It's like whoever is on the other side of that door is pathological. Because they won't stop ringing your bell. Okay. Don't freak out.

Leslie must have watched a ton of horror movies, because she was totally freaking out. She was starting to freak me out. I tried to look through the peephole, but I wasn't quite tall enough.

LESLIE: Could it be your grandma?
ME: No. All my grandparents are dead.
LESLIE: That's so tragic. Okay. Are you looking through the peephole yet?
ME: I can't see anything that way. I have to look out the window.
LESLIE: Okay. Keep talking really loudly into the phone so they don't think you're alone.

That was a good idea. So I yelled.

ME: I am pretty tired from our kung fu class. What about you? Maybe we should feed the dogs and go to bed.

LESLIE: You are great at having fake conversations. What do you see?

As quietly as I could, I moved the curtain in the front window and tried to take a very quick peek.

ME: It looks like a girl.

But instead of an answer from Leslie, all I heard was silence. I kept reporting what I saw into the phone anyway. "She's about my height. And she has a duffel bag."

I stared at the girl outside my house. "She looks familiar. Wait. It might be my cousin. Angelina?" I said.

"Lane!" the voice cheered. "I thought I saw you peeking out the window. Open up! After two plane flights, I'm finally here!"

This didn't make sense. Why was Angelina by herself? "Where are my parents?"

She shrugged. "They didn't pick me up. I had to take a taxi."

Since Leslie was completely nonresponsive, I ended the call and slid my phone in my pocket.

"They're at the airport right now," I explained.

"Oh," Angelina said. "I arrived two hours ago. And just waited."

I stared at my cousin underneath the yellow puddle of light made by our porch lamp. She didn't look at all like I remembered her. She had long dark hair and bright pink lips, and her eyes were basically the greenest eyes I'd ever seen in my life. Greener than the eyes of Rachel's Siamese cat, Petunia. There was no doubt about it, Angelina looked cute.

"Can you let me in?" Angelina asked. "I've had a long day."

And since she was my cousin, I unlocked the dead bolt and opened the door. The first thing I noticed when she walked inside was her clothes. Her pants looked either stained or painted, and her shirt had a picture of a mean dog on it. Then I noticed that her mouth looked really small. Not to get all judge-y, but it was incredibly tiny. She probably had to visit a special dentist who had undersized hands.

Angelina set her duffel bag down and gave me a huge hug. "It is so great to see you!"

I did not return that compliment. I said, "We should probably call my parents."

"I already tried," Angelina said. "Your mom didn't answer."

That didn't sound like my mom at all. She kept her phone's volume turned up to the max, and she always picked up every call. Even telemarketers. So I pulled my phone back out and dialed her up.

ME: Mom—

MOM: I can't talk right now. We can't find Angelina.
    She took an earlier flight in her connecting city.
    They've lost her!

ME: She's here.

MOM: What? How?

ME: She waited for two hours and then took a taxi.

MOM: Thank goodness! This is the best news I've
    heard all year. We're on our way.

I was surprised to hear my mother say that it was the best news she'd heard all year. Because I'd told her a bunch of newsworthy stuff that I thought ranked much higher.

"Can I get you anything to eat?" I asked. "Are you hungry?"

Angelina shook her head. "I bought a shrimp dinner at the airport."

That was an interesting choice. I would have bought pizza or ice cream. It wouldn't even have occurred to me to buy a shrimp dinner.

"I think I'm ready for bed," Angelina said.

"Um," I said. "Maybe we should wait for my parents? They'll probably want to say hi to you and stuff."

Angelina sat down in the wingback chair I was writing my poem about.

"I feel eighty percent dead," she said. "I wasn't built to fly."

The more I looked at her, the more I noticed her weird dog shirt. It was sort of frightening. Like maybe it had rabies.

"Do you want to watch TV?" I asked.

She shook her head. "I don't really watch TV. Do you mind if I give myself a quick tour?"

"Um," I said. It seemed weird to request to snoop around my house by herself. But before I could tell her a good reason to stay put, Leslie called me back. "I have to take this call," I told Angelina.

"No problemo," my cousin said cheerily, flashing me a thumbs-up sign.

"Did you hang up on me?" Leslie asked.

"I don't think so," I told her. I watched Angelina wandering through the living room, pausing in front of our framed family photos. "It was my cousin."

"Lane, you totally should have told me you were expecting a cousin. You gave me a serious freak-out."

"She's unexpected," I said. But then I worried that wasn't the right thing to say. Because my mom wanted Angelina to appear very expected. And permanent at my school.

"Okay," Leslie said. "I gotta jam or I'll miss my movie. Don't forget the vegan cookies. Hope your cousin isn't a drag! Later."

I had no idea that Leslie was so spastic. When I walked into the living room to talk to Angelina, she wasn't there anymore. "Angelina?" I called.

"I'm checking out the kitchen," she said.

I walked into kitchen, but she wasn't there.

"Angelina?" I called.

"Now I'm in the garage!"

She sure seemed comfortable in my house. As I headed toward the garage, my phone buzzed and I saw that I had a message from Todd. It was so exciting.

Todd: Is your cousin there yet?

That was not a very exciting message.

Me: Yes. In my garage.

Angelina reentered the house and popped through the doorway to the kitchen. "Who are you texting?"

I shrugged. She didn't need to know who I was texting.

"Do you want me to try to guess?" Angelina asked. Her face lit up with excitement and she sat down at the kitchen table.

But I didn't want her to guess. I wanted her to stop being so nosy. "It's just a friend," I said.

My phone buzzed again. I loved seeing Todd's name light up.

Todd: Can you send a picture?
Me: Of what?
Todd: Her!

What? No way. Why would he want to see a picture of Angelina?

Me: No.

Buzz! Buzz! Buzz!

Todd: I'm at Jagger's. We want to see what she looks like.

"What are you and your friend texting about?" Angelina asked.

Were all people from Alaska this intrusive? Rather than lie or dodge everything, I decided it was easier to answer honestly. "My friend Todd wants me to send him a picture of you."

"Ooh," Angelina said. "Is your friend Todd cute?"

What? Was my cousin crazy?

"Um," I said. "You are asking too many questions."

"You're right," Angelina said, popping out of the chair. "Okay. My left is my good side. How should I pose?"

This was so weird. I couldn't believe that I had to send my secret boyfriend a photo of my Alaskan cousin's good side while she posed. But I didn't see a better option. As soon as I had her focused in the frame I realized her dog shirt looked super creepy, and so I chose to take a close-up of just her face. *Click!*

"Okay," Angelina said. "Now we should send him a picture of both of us."

"That's not really necessary," I said. Because Todd already knew exactly what I looked like. I was pretty sure he thought I was cute and that was part of why he liked me.

"It's totally necessary," Angelina said, taking my phone and holding it at arm's length from us. "We will never repeat this moment. It should be recorded." *Click.*

"You need to count to three," I said. "My eyes were closed."

Angelina and I both looked at the picture. She had a great smile, and if you cropped out everything below the neck, she looked cute enough to be a model on the cover of a teen magazine. For some reason, in addition to having half-open eyes, I seemed to have discolored skin, as if I was green.

"The lamp muddied your light. Do you want to take another one?" Angelina asked.

I shook my head.

"Are you going to send your friend the first picture or the second one?" Angelina asked.

"The first one," I said. There was no way I was sending Todd a picture of me looking sleepy, green, and ugly. And then, right as I was sending it, my parents came home.

"Unbelievable!" my mother said as she hurried in the front door. "How could they let you board an earlier flight and not notify me?"

Angelina shrugged. "They just did."

"Luckily, all our complaining got us a free voucher for another ticket, so you can come visit us again," my dad said.

"So cool!" Angelina said. Then she raced over and hugged him.

"Angelina," he said as he returned her hug for, like, forty-seven seconds. "Forget the rocky start. We are so excited to have you as a guest. Make yourself at home. *Mi casa es su casa*. Right, Lane?"

I was surprised at this statement for several reasons. First, when did he become the kind of person who returned hugs for forty-seven seconds? Second, when did *we* as a family decide any of these things? And lastly, when did my dad start speaking Spanish? I'd never even heard him say *adios* or *amigo*. *Mi casa es su casa?* When my dad wanted to say crazy things in a foreign language he usually chose German. *Bis bald! Danke! Mach's gut.*

"Yes," my mother encouraged her. "He's right. For the next month I have two daughters." I watched as she sappily scooped a beaming Angelina into her arms.

My stomach flipped. Were my parents losing their minds? I understood that we needed to make Angelina comfortable. But I didn't think we needed to convince her she was my sister. Not to be rude. But Angelina Mint Taravel didn't exactly look like sister material. She was more like a special project. Maybe a broken doll you find in the street and you take it home and fix it up and then give it to somebody else. The doll gets a second life. And you feel really good about yourself for taking pity on a broken doll in the first place.

"You guys are the best," Angelina said. And then she walked over and wrapped her arms around me and hugged me. And I hugged her back a little, but I also held back. Because in addition to having boundaries, I also wasn't sappy.

"I've never had a sister!" Angelina said.

Hearing this made everything feel extra dreadful.

"Aren't you going to say anything to Angelina?" my mom asked.

It felt as if she wanted me to declare that I considered Angelina my sister. No way. Not happening. So I said something else. I asked a practical question.

"Where are all your suitcases?" Because I didn't see anything besides a duffel bag. Had she come with only a duffel bag? Didn't she own cute clothes? Where were they? Not on her.

"I only brought what I need," Angelina said.

All three of us stared at her bag. That contained everything she needed for a month?

"I'm sure if you forgot something, Lane can lend you whatever you need," my mom said.

This was not ideal news.

"I am so tired," Angelina said. "I think I'm ready for bed."

"Of course!" my mother agreed. "Lane will show you to her room."

Suddenly, I felt very burdened. Angelina Mint Taravel was my sole responsibility. Like an exchange student. Or a high-needs dog. She'd been deposited into my care, and now it was my job to look after her and show her EVERYTHING.

As I led Angelina down the hallway to my room, she began to whistle. And something about the pitch of that sound made the hair on my arms stand up. It was as if I knew on some level what was coming. As if I understood that *my life* was no longer going to be *my life*.

· 6 ·

I sort of assumed that Angelina would just sleep in her dog shirt. I figured that she was traveling in stuff that was almost pajamas anyway. But that wasn't what happened. As soon as we got to my room, Angelina asked if she could borrow a coat hanger. I gave her one right away, because I had a pile of about a dozen on my floor.

"Unpacking?" I asked. I was curious to see what clothes she'd brought from Alaska. But instead of opening up her bag, she took off her weird T-shirt and put it on the hanger. I was relieved to see that she was also wearing a bra.

"I'm wearing this to school the first day," Angelina said, hoisting the shirt above us. "Do you think all the wrinkles will fall out by then?"

I gasped a little. She shouldn't have been worried about whether the wrinkles would fall out over the weekend.

First, she should have worried about whether it smelled. My mom used dryer sheets, so all our clothes smelled like baby powder, and we only wore our clothes once and then tossed them in the hamper. Didn't Angelina's family follow that rule too? Second, she should have been worried about how weird and ugly her shirt would look to people at my school. But as soon as I thought these things, I felt bad for judging Angelina. I mean, maybe it was a picture of her dog on the front. Maybe she was homesick and so she thought wearing his photo would improve her mood. I pointed to the awful-looking gray dog on the front. "Is he your dog?"

Angelina gave me a confused look and shook her head. "It's a wolf."

I glanced at her shirt again. She was right. That weird dog did look like a wolf. And there was also a giant full moon on it.

"Oh," I said. "You don't want to show up in your wolf shirt. Nobody in my school wears those."

I thought Angelina's smile would fall right off her face. But it didn't. It stayed there. "Ooh. So I'd be the first?"

That was when I suspected that teaching Angelina how to act like a normal sixth grader and make friends at Rio Chama Middle School was going to be pretty difficult.

"I don't think that's a good idea," I said. "People at my school wear plain T-shirts. I mean, sometimes they have stripes or a pocket on them. But not wild beasts."

"Interesting," Angelina said.

"I have plenty of shirts I can lend you," I offered, even

though I didn't really want to lend her my clothes. I didn't even lend them to my friends. We each had our own style, so we didn't really share.

Angelina kept staring at her wolf shirt like she was in love with it.

"I'm having some friends over tomorrow night for a sleepover," I said. "We can have a fashion show. My friend Ava will bring over a ton of clothes for you to try on."

"How many friends?" Angelina asked.

"Ava, Rachel, and Lucia," I said.

"That's cool," Angelina said. "I *love* meeting new people."

I looked at her duffel bag again. "Anything else you want to unpack?"

"Just three things," she said.

I watched her unzip the bag. I was dying to see what was inside it. But she didn't open it all the way. She just pulled out a tank top and a small notebook and a toothbrush.

"My pajama top and my diary and my toothbrush," she explained.

Her pajama top looked almost normal. Except it had weird ink stains on it.

"I'll be right back," she said.

"You can't leave my room wearing just a bra!" I said.

Angelina's face look horrified. "I know that."

She slid her inky pajama top over her head and ran out of my room. And then she returned.

"Where's your bathroom?" she asked.

"Across the hallway," I said. I followed her. "Don't use the toothpaste in the blue tube. It's got special foaming action for people with sensitive teeth."

"It's okay if Angelina wants to use my toothpaste," my dad called.

I couldn't believe he was eavesdropping on us.

"Use the plain white tube," I said. "It tastes better. And it's less expensive."

"I have *so* much to learn," Angelina said as she slammed the bathroom door.

Then, as if she was competing in the tooth-brushing Olympics, she swung the bathroom door open about five seconds later. "Finished!"

I didn't bother to ask her if she'd flossed. We went back to my room and Angelina turned down the blanket on the left side of my queen bed. She'd taken off her bra in the bathroom, and she placed the carefully folded square of straps and cotton cups on the table beside my bed. I climbed into my spot and kept my night-light on so she wouldn't stub her toe on anything if she had to get up.

"Do you want me to keep the light on for you?" I asked. This wasn't ideal, because I needed total darkness to sleep. But I figured on her first night after having lived through so many solo adventures, I should let her write in her journal.

"It's okay. My diary has a built-in light," she said.

What?

When she got in bed next to me, she opened her diary and a tiny light popped on. I knew it was rude to watch her scribble, but I couldn't help myself.

"I'm almost done," Angelina said. "Just want to capture the conversation I had with the cabdriver before I forget it. Diego had some wise guidance."

This was so weird.

"Done!" Angelina said, slamming the book closed. As soon as she rolled over, I felt her tug the covers a little bit, which didn't thrill me. I really didn't enjoy sleeping with a cover-tugger.

"Night," I said.

"Night," she said.

I turned off my light and nearly screamed. There was a creepy glow coming from my closet. Then I realized what it was. "Does your wolf shirt glow in the dark?"

"Yeah."

Poor Angelina. She was just too weird. Clearly, the next month was going to be brutal. And what was my job in all this? Was I supposed to be some sort of friendship lifeline for her? Or a public-humiliation shield? Since I was class captain, I had clout, but should I waste it all on Angelina? Shouldn't I waste it on myself? And my friends?

Sixth grade was under way and running like a well-oiled machine. How would Angelina find her place? Would she make friends? Would she be teased? Would she perform well on our frequent vocabulary exams? Would she end up having at least two cute shirts in her duffel bag? I had so many questions. But zero answers.

On the verge of sleep, I turned and looked at Angelina one last time. Poor Angelina. In the dim light of evening, with her choppy bangs pasted to her sweaty forehead, she

looked very much like a geek. *Blink. Yawn. Blink. Yawn. Blink.*
I highly doubted daylight could improve this situation.

Buzz. Buzz. Buzz.

I grabbed my phone and looked at the message.

Todd: Jagger thinks she's cute.

I stared at my phone in disbelief. And then Todd sent a
second message.

Todd: We want to crash your sleepover!

On a normal day, that would have been thrilling news.
But today was not a normal day. Then I did something that
I had never done in the history of owning my phone. I de-
leted a message from Todd Romero. *Jagger thinks she's cute.* I
plunked the message right in the trash, where it belonged.
Plink. It didn't matter, I reassured myself. Angelina was
only here for a month. And once Jagger met her, he'd see
that she wasn't *that* cute. He'd be way better off with Ava.

· 7 ·

I was fairly certain Angelina would crash and burn without my social guidance.

The next right at my sleepover, as soon as Angelina was out of earshot, I asked my friends what they thought of her.

"She's sort of fascinating," Lucia said.

"She has cute hair," Rachel added.

"She is *W-E-I-R-D*," Ava said.

"Shhh," I said. "Be quieter with your insults."

We were all waiting for Angelina to join us on the trampoline, anticipating her makeover. We weren't aggressive about it. Nobody wanted to cut her hair or smear her face with a bunch of makeup. We were only interested in improving her wardrobe.

Then the screen door creaked and we all watched Angelina slide it open. As an experiment, we'd given her a pair of Ava's triple-soft, hand-dyed pajamas, which she'd bought at a boutique in Tucson. We'd informed Angelina that the theme of the trampoline party was a pj swap, so everybody had to switch pj's. It was a total lie. But we needed to get Angelina comfortable with the idea that our clothes were better than her clothes and that in order to establish a decent reputation she should start wearing them immediately.

I crawled to the side of the trampoline so I could get the best possible view of Angelina. She walked onto the porch wearing a short-sleeved cotton top that circled her waist in ruffles. Both the top and shorts were multiple shades of green, and the bottoms were looped with a ribbon belt. Ever since Ava had shown me the pajamas, I'd been worried that Angelina would look like a forest and the pattern would swallow her. But it didn't. What a relief. Angelina looked so cute.

"Green is really your color!" Rachel said. "It makes your skin look less pale."

"The ruffles make your eyes pop," Lucia said.

"Your torso looks great belted," Ava added.

I cheerfully lowered my head. Maybe helping her wouldn't require a ton of my time and effort. Things looked like they could turn out okay, because when you put normal clothes on her, Angelina looked like one of us. These realizations made me feel much more mellow about introducing Angelina to everybody I knew. She bounced down the steps and hopped onto the middle of the trampoline, making our sleeping bags slide to the center.

Rachel squealed like she liked it. So Angelina bounced us again.

"Stop!" Ava screamed. "I'm fragile!"

But Angelina didn't stop. "I'm going to crack you!"

Whoa. That seemed hostile. And a little immature. We'd stopped playing crack the egg in fourth grade. Right after Lucia stepped on Ava's ankle.

"No!" Ava said. "We don't play that game!"

But Angelina didn't stop. She bounced us very high.

"I'm cracked!" Lucia said, unfolding her legs.

"I'm double cracked!" Rachel said, falling onto her side.

"I'm not playing," Ava said.

"Okay, Angelina," I said. "Let's sit."

"In Alaska, we play this game for days," Angelina said.

Ava looked horrified.

"But we have our stuff on the trampoline," I explained. "We don't want to break anything."

"Yeah," Ava added. "If my phone gets damaged, I'll die."

"Okay," Angelina said. "I don't want to wreck anybody's phone." And so she did sit, but not before she released one more powerful bounce and landed hard on her butt in front of us. The force of that bounce made Ava topple onto her side.

"Seriously, Angelina," Ava said, springing back up to a sitting position. "We don't play that game anymore for a reason."

"I know," Angelina said, frowning big. "You're fragile and your phone could break."

"And we've got secret visitors coming over and you've ruined everybody's hair!" Ava pointed to her mess of a blond bob. Normally, it was very smooth. At the present time, not so much.

"Shhh," I said. Other than the five of us on the trampoline, I didn't want anyone else to know that Todd and Jagger were going to crash our pajama party. My parents would flip. The whole point of the party was to introduce Angelina to a few of my friends before she started school. If we were caught with boys, my parents would ground me for weeks, and then be disappointed in me for eons.

"Will I get to meet Todd Romero?" Angelina whispered. "Your boyfriend?"

Rachel giggled.

"I knew it!" Lucia said.

I hadn't told them either of them that Todd was almost my boyfriend. So I was furious that Angelina had said anything.

"Shut up!" I said. I could feel myself blushing. "And, Angelina, don't call him my boyfriend ever again."

I glared at Ava, because I figured she must have accidentally told Angelina. But Ava looked at me as if she was pretty surprised.

"Oh," Angelina said. "Don't get mad at Ava. She didn't tell me. You talk in your sleep. I think you have a recurring dream that you go to the beach with him. Because all last night, you kept telling Todd Romero to stop splashing you."

Rachel giggled again. This was awful. I didn't want

my friends to know that I dreamed about Todd Romero splashing me!

That was when Ava stood up for me. She aimed her finger at Angelina and shook it in her face. "It's rude to repeat what people say in their dreams. I mean, it's totally against girl code."

Angelina lowered her head like she felt bad and apologetic. "I didn't mean to be rude. I just can't believe you have a boyfriend."

I couldn't hold in my frustration. "Shhh. Stop talking about this right now."

"Nobody heard us," Lucia said. "It's okay."

But it was not okay. Because people had heard—Lucia and Rachel. "No more!"

"Can I ask you a question?" Angelina whispered. Her voice sounded sad and filled with regret.

"I guess," I huffed.

"What's girl code?" she asked.

That was when Lucia, Rachel, Ava, and I all gasped in disbelief. We knew Angelina was clueless when it came to clothes and trends. But we had no idea she was clueless when it came to girl code.

"Girl code is the bond by which we live," Ava said as she smoothed her hair and sat up very straight.

"It means friends are more important than anything," Lucia said.

"It means we treat each other like sisters," Rachel said. "And we keep each others' secrets."

"Also," Ava said, "we don't crush on the same guy."

"Oh," Angelina said. "That sounds reasonable. I can do that."

Knowing what I knew, I really hoped she could.

It startled me to hear a crunching sound. But when I looked up, I saw my mom in her bathrobe walking across the lawn toward us.

"You're sure you want to stay out all night?" she asked.

"Totally," I said. Because that was the only way Todd and Jagger could crash our pj party.

"If you want to come inside for any reason, use this flashlight." She handed me a mini light that she'd given me to take camping.

I tucked it inside my sleeping bag.

"So when are Todd and Jagger coming?" Angelina asked.

"Shhh," I said. My mom wasn't even back inside the house yet. "Don't ruin this for us."

"Yeah," Ava said. "Zip it."

"Sorry," Angelina said. "I didn't realize I was being loud."

"Well, you were," Ava said.

"Okay. Let's drop this and look at the stars," Lucia said.

I thought that was a pretty good idea. After settling into our sleeping bags, we stared up into the sky.

"Is it weird that I see squids when I do this?" Rachel asked.

"No," I said. I didn't want Rachel to think she was weird.

"There's Ursa Major. And there's the North Star. And I think that's Venus," Lucia said.

It was a dark and cloudless night in Santa Fe and the stars shone brightly. I concentrated on the tip of Lucia's pointer finger. All the smaller stars winked at us while we hunted for the famous ones.

"How did you learn all the names of the stars and where to find them?" Angelina asked.

"My dad told me," Lucia said. "We stargaze all the time. We think it's fun to look for nebulae together."

Angelina didn't ask any follow-up questions. And the silence that followed while we stared into the starry sky made me feel a little bit sad for my cousin.

· 8 ·

I was very lucky that Todd Romero and Jagger Evenson were so sneaky. Under the cover of darkness, late in the night, they crawled beneath the trampoline and lay in the grass. Todd reached up with his finger and poked the mesh near my face.

"I'm here," Todd whispered.

"Hey," Jagger said.

I couldn't believe I'd fallen asleep. I'd been so excited that they were going to sneak over that I'd tried to stay up as long as I could. But at some point I'd surrendered to sleep while staring at the dark sky filled with sparkling stars, and conked out.

"Hi," Angelina whispered. "I'm Lane's cousin, Angelina. My mom is her mom's sister. We were born five days apart. But I'm an Aquarius, and Lane's a Virgo."

I wanted to die. Why was Angelina telling Todd and Jagger that I was a Virgo? And why did it matter that she was an Aquarius? And why was she talking about our family tree? Couldn't she have just introduced herself as my cousin? Wasn't that what normal sixth graders did? And why wasn't she as groggy as I was?

"You're from Alaska, right?" Todd asked.

"Yeah," Angelina said. "I'm from a town called Eagle River near Anchorage."

I wanted to interrupt this conversation, but I wasn't sure how to do it.

"Cool," Todd said. "How many eagles have you seen?"

By now, Lucia and Rachel and Ava were up and we were all staring down through the mesh at Todd and Jagger.

"Eagles are so common in Alaska that I see at least three or four every day," Angelina explained.

"Wow," Jagger said. "You mean, like, bald eagles?"

"Yes," Angelina said. "I mean bald eagles."

"Have you ever seen a bear?" Todd asked.

"I have," Angelina said. "In the forest near my house there are fifty-two tagged brown bears and so many black bears that they don't even bother to tag them. And there are wolves too."

"Awesome," Jagger said.

"Hi, Jagger," Ava said. "I like your jacket."

I squinted to get a better look at Jagger's jacket. In the darkness, all that I could tell was that it looked blue.

"Thanks," Jagger said.

"What time is it?" Rachel asked, sounding groggy.

"Time for donuts?" Todd asked.

I watched as Todd pulled a bright white box from a paper bag and gently shook it.

"You are so sweet," Ava cooed.

"Ooh," Rachel said. "Do any of them have jelly centers?"

Todd opened the box and peeked inside. "You'll have to look for yourself."

"Hand it over," Rachel said.

I think I heard her stomach growl. In addition to drawing squids, Rachel's other favorite pastime was eating anything with sugar in it.

"You have to come and get it," Todd said.

"But the grass is covered in dew," Lucia said.

She was so practical.

Todd shook the box again. "I'm going to count to ten. You better get them."

Jagger laughed. "If you don't, I'll eat 'em."

"No!" Rachel said.

"Shhh," I said. The last thing I needed was to get caught with my almost boyfriend bringing donuts to my pj party.

"Can't you just hand them to us?" Lucia asked.

And then, before I could figure out a way to flirt with Todd and persuade him to give us the donuts, something terrible happened. Angelina ruined my moment.

"I'll risk the dew," she said.

With the speed of a wild dog and the flexibility of a monkey, Angelina hooked her legs on the metal frame of the trampoline and lowered herself to the grass. "Hand them over." She reached her arms toward my almost boyfriend. And he surrendered the box right away.

"You're quick," Jagger said.

"Alarmingly quick," Ava said.

Angelina swung herself back onto the trampoline and handed Rachel the box. "There is a jelly-filled donut!" she squealed.

I watched in horror as the kitchen light flicked on.

"You better scram," Lucia said.

"Thanks for the donuts," Angelina said.

My big, exciting moment with Todd had suddenly turned to trash. We should have been able to hang out and talk to each other for hours. Maybe he would have even climbed on the trampoline with me. But before I could even come up with a good place for them to hide, Todd Romero and Jagger Evenson were absolutely gone. I watched my mother wave to us from the kitchen window. What a bummer. I waved back to her. And so did my friends. Angelina waved so much that it looked like she was trying to fend off a vicious mosquito.

"That was so lame," Ava said.

"Why?" Angelina asked. "Don't you like donuts?"

It was tragic how clueless Angelina could be. Mostly tragic for me and Todd. But also tragic for her. How would she make friends and survive for a month at Rio Chama Middle School? It was going to be tough.

"Getting the donuts was lame," Ava said. "You stole

Lane's thunder. And it's weird to talk about your zodiac sign with guys until you're much older. Like when you're in college."

"Yeah," Rachel said as she bit into a donut that released a small stream of red jelly down her finger. "That did feel a little weird."

"Oh," Angelina said.

"You really hijacked the guys," Ava said.

"Hijack?" Angelina said. "Did I hijack somebody?" She turned toward me when she asked the question.

"Yeah," Ava said. "They were here to see Lane. And me. And we barely got to talk to them."

"Sorry," Angelina said. "I didn't mean to do that."

"Let's call it an honest mistake and go to bed," Lucia said. "It's late."

But I didn't feel like going to bed. I felt like being mad at Angelina. And so did Ava.

"Sixth grade isn't a joke at Rio Chama Middle School," Ava said. "There are important rules to follow."

Angelina looked scared.

"Don't freak her out," Rachel said. "You'll be fine. Probably."

"Don't lie to her," Ava said. "She's poised for geekdom!"

"I doubt she'll get branded as a geek," Lucia said. "Her hair is very nongeek."

I thought about how her choppy bangs looked pasted to her sweaty forehead. She better not let her forehead get sweaty at school.

Angelina stared at her donut but didn't take another bite. "Thanks."

"Her hair needs to have a style. It can't be loose like a wild animal. And she needs to wear clothes that help her blend. Blending will be critical to your social success," Ava told her.

"I don't care if I blend," Angelina said.

Ava stared at her. "You better."

And even though Ava was speaking to Angelina in a harsh way, I didn't interrupt her, because I thought that everything Ava was saying was basically true.

"Don't you want to make friends? Don't you want to avoid the geeks and mingle with cool kids? Why come here and have a nightmare experience?" Ava asked.

Angelina blinked. Four times. She looked as if she wasn't totally sure if she cared or not.

"Is our school *that* bad?" Rachel asked.

"When it comes to being the new girl, any school can be *that* bad," Ava said.

"Right," Angelina said as she nervously twirled her ribbon belt around her finger.

None of us said anything. We just stared at Angelina while she thought and thought. I didn't understand what was so hard about blending. If I were as weird as Angelina, I would have been thrilled to try to show up at a new place and blend.

"This problem is easy to solve," Lucia said. "Just borrow some of Lane's clothes and don't talk too much about bald eagles and you'll be fine."

"You can probably talk a little bit about grizzly bears," Rachel said.

Lucia and Ava and I shot Rachel some disapproving looks. She was not helping.

"I need a glass of water," Angelina said. "My donut is sticking to my throat."

I gave her my flashlight and we watched as she walked barefoot through the grass toward the house.

"She's different," Rachel said. "Maybe people will like that."

We all looked at Rachel again. Had her jelly donut made her crazy?

"She's *too* different," Ava said. "Plus, she's weird. She'll sink Lane's popularity faster than a harpoon takes down a whale."

"No way," Rachel said. "Lane is class captain."

"That's right," Ava said. "She'll be planning the most amazing parties our school has ever seen. People are expecting a lot out of her now."

That statement felt heavy and made me hold my breath. While I'd thought about the parties, I hadn't really thought about other people's expectations.

"I'm sure everything will be fine," I said in a very shaky voice.

"I'm sure a whale thinks that right before it gets harpooned," Ava snapped.

"Stop!" Lucia said. "I actually saw a show about whaling ships, and it takes a long time for a harpoon to tire a whale."

"Whatever," Ava said. "Eventually the whale sinks. And Lane shouldn't be a harpooned whale. She deserves so much more than that."

I really agreed with Ava's position on this.

"But the whale doesn't sink," Lucia said. "It's cut up into useful parts. For lamp oil and stuff."

"That's an even worse fate than sinking!" Ava said. "Listen, here's the plan. On Monday, if Angelina shows up at school looking decent and acting normal, we'll befriend her and do what we can to help her survive. But if she doesn't listen to us and she shows up refusing to blend, we need to cut her loose and let her swim those waters alone."

There was a bunch of silence. I think we were all thinking about the cut-up whale.

"That's so harsh," Rachel said finally. "I feel bad for her."

"Her? Feel bad for *us*. We can't hang out with a weirdo. People will think we're weird too."

"So we're just going to ditch my cousin?" I asked.

Ava clicked her tongue. "If you want a happy future that includes Todd Romero, yeah. We ditch her."

It took Angelina a long time to come back to the trampoline. And when she did, I tried not to look at her too much. I knew what I had to do. I just hoped I'd be able to do it.

· 9 ·

I made my two dozen cookies on Sunday night. I settled on a raw vegan chocolate chip recipe. My mom voiced some concern over the fact that we didn't have to bake them, but I thought that was a time-saving bonus. With my raw cookies, all I had to do was leave them out and dehydrate them for the night.

"What are these for, again?" Angelina asked as she watched me scoop the last mound of dough onto a piece of parchment paper.

"A cookie basket," I said. Angelina needed to start accepting the fact that I didn't have to exhaustively answer every single one of her questions.

"And you're not concerned that they look a little bit like dog poop?" she asked.

I stared at my undehydrated cookies. "They taste

awesome," I said, acting as if her dog poop comparison hadn't offended me. Because I didn't think they looked like that at all. I thought they looked vegan-y.

"Are you going to bed right now?" Angelina asked, trailing behind me to the bathroom.

It was starting to feel like I had a stalker. "Yeah."

"My mom might call me tonight. It depends on what time her ship makes port," she said. "So I'm going to stay up."

"Okay," I said. I tried to imagine what it would feel like if my mom had boarded a ship and sailed off for a month. But I couldn't wrap my mind around it. No matter how bad my mom wanted to visit a foreign country or take a vacation, she would never do that.

I entered my bedroom and noticed that Angelina still hadn't laid out her outfit for school like I'd suggested. It drove me nuts that I didn't know what she was going to wear tomorrow. And I couldn't tell if she was intentionally trying to drive me nuts or if it was an accidental thing. Maybe I should mention that I was willing to help her pick out an outfit one more time?

Rather than reach out to her, I shut the door instead. It wasn't my job to dress my cousin.

"Night!" Angelina called to me. "I'll make sure nobody eats your cookies."

Who did she think was going to eat my cookies? "Okay," I said. And I pulled out my pink bohemian tunic top and my favorite pair of jeans so they'd be ready for me to wear tomorrow.

* * *

I wasn't prepared for the drama. Before the sun even made it up, the first day of school with Angelina started with a curveball.

"Would it be a bad idea for me to wear Ava's pajamas to school?"

I almost fell over when Angelina asked me this.

"Uh, yeah. It would be a terrible idea," I answered. I was basically all dressed, and had thought Angelina was on board to wear my cute periwinkle shirt with puffy sleeves. Ten minutes ago, when she'd tried it on, we'd both agreed that she looked great in it.

"That's too bad," Angelina said. "Because I really like the ribbon belt."

Upon hearing this, I ran to my closet and pulled out every belt I owned. Thin. Thick. Beaded. Braided. "Take your pick," I said. "Belts and beyond." It surprised me how quickly I was willing to surrender my entire wardrobe to Angelina. Probably, I was motivated by guilt. I felt bad knowing that chances were good that if Angelina dressed in her own clothes, she would wind up looking so dweeby that I would have to ditch her. Was it wrong to want to arrive at school with two dozen vegan cookies and a cousin who looked regular? Seriously. Was it wrong to want that?

Many freaky things happened that morning before Angelina and I made it to school. First, my mom made us a special egg breakfast with waffles on the side, which she never did except for random Sundays when we had guests. Second, my dad joined us. Typically, he was already headed to work and rarely ate breakfast with us, because when you supervise a groundskeeping crew on a college campus, apparently you have to sweep all the paths clear and remove all tripping hazards before classes start.

But the freakiest thing had to be that Angelina had chosen to wear her wolf T-shirt to my school on her first day. Inside out! She looked ridiculous. Was she trying to hide the fact that her T-shirt had a wolf on it? Because even inside out, you could clearly see the outline of that beast. I thought people might think she was trying to hide a stain. And then maybe these same people would think she didn't have enough money to buy an unstained ugly shirt. I could tell that my mom and dad weren't thrilled with her fashion choice. But they didn't make her change. It was crazy. I think they still felt bad that she had to take a taxi to our house from the airport. Clearly, Angelina was going to be able to get away with murder the entire month she lived with me. It was like the worst thing that had ever happened to me kept getting worse. Like a scrape that gets infected because bacteria gets into it.

"Why don't I drive you to school?" my dad said.

At first I was going to tell him no thanks. But the thought of boarding my school bus with Angelina made me feel queasy.

"Okay," I said.

"And your health cookies are ready to go. I put them in a plastic box," my mom said, lifting a see-through box off the counter and then setting it back down.

"They're vegan cookies, not health cookies," I explained.

"Did the same teacher who told you to write a poem about the couch tell you to make vegan cookies?" my dad asked.

My dad didn't understand how my school worked at all. "No," I said, without bothering to explain more. I glanced at my mom, because it looked as if she had more to say.

"I packed you each a lunch with ham-and-cheese sandwiches in case you don't like what they're serving today," my mom said.

That didn't make sense. Our cafeteria had a ton of choices. And today was pizza Monday. My mom knew I loved pizza Monday.

"It's pizza Monday," I said.

"I love ham-and-cheese sandwiches," Angelina said. "Did my mom tell you that?"

"I just want to make sure you have a great first day," my mom said.

"Who doesn't like pizza?" I mumbled. But nobody responded. I probably didn't mumble loud enough.

I watched as Angelina loaded her waffle with two different flavors of jam. Then she added honey! And sprinkled raisins on it! Where did she get raisins? We didn't have any in our house. My dad and I *hated* raisins. She must have brought them with her from Alaska. That was weird. My mom and dad and I ate our eggs and waffles the way normal people did: salted and peppered, and syruped.

I'm sure my dad said many interesting things as he drove Angelina and me to our doom. But I don't really remember them. All I remember are the last words he said as I climbed out of the car. Angelina had already gotten out and was doing some weird arm stretches near the trunk.

"She's a little different," my dad said. "Watch out for her. Protect her. She's your flesh and blood."

I glanced at her in her jacket. Once she took it off and revealed her inside-out wolf T-shirt I didn't know how I could protect her.

"Everyone is going to see she's a total geek," I whispered. "I *really* hate this."

My dad nodded. "I like your attitude. Angelina is totally neat. And everyone will see how *really* great she is!"

He had to be kidding. But he didn't look like he was kidding. Had he misheard me? How could he confuse "I *really* hate this" with "how *really* great she is"? How could he think I thought that Angelina was "neat"? I wanted to correct him, but my father looked incredibly serious and ridiculously proud of me. "Not everybody who looks at Angelina sees what we see. You're an impressive kid. I'm glad you're mine."

I could not believe my morning. My dad blinked at me very lovingly and it looked as if he was about to cry. In the parking lot! So I said what I thought I needed to say to make him stop. "Thanks. I'll make sure Angelina has an awesome day."

Then I grabbed Angelina by the arm and sped her up the walkway toward my school's front doors.

"You are so eager to learn!" she said.

"We need to get to the bathroom," I said under my breath. I knew what I had to do.

We got to the bathroom and I made Angelina enter the same stall as me.

"Are you sick?" she asked.

I didn't quite know how to answer that. So I unleashed a flood of honesty. "Angelina, if you wear that shirt, you won't make a single friend. People will brand you a major loser and maybe even throw food at you in the cafeteria. They usually serve breadsticks on pizza Monday, and those are pretty easy to aim. Please. Please. Please. I'm class captain. I can't have a loser for a cousin. Please."

She looked at me with big, surprised eyes. "But it's the only shirt I have with me."

This was a problem. Why hadn't I thought to bring my periwinkle shirt as a spare? Angelina reached for the door.

"No," I said.

She stopped. "What?" she asked.

I knew what I needed to do.

I pulled off my pink bohemian tunic and pushed it into Angelina's stomach. I would wear her wolf shirt. Just like my father wanted, I would protect her. I, Lane Cisco, would look like the geek.

As I stood in my bra, dreading the morning bell, I realized this was the most vulnerable I'd ever felt. "Give me your shirt."

"All right. If you insist," she said.

I knew I was making a mistake the second I slid that T-shirt over my head. I didn't even bother putting it on inside out. "Can I borrow your jacket too?" I asked. I slipped on her jacket right away and zipped it up so that nobody would see I was wearing a glowing wolf head. Once Angelina had put on my pink shirt she looked cute and normal. It was crazy how much one piece of clothing could transform this girl.

"Time for Mr. Guzman's class," I said, tugging on her arm a little.

But she didn't follow me. "I need to fix my hair," she said.

That was a bad idea. Her hair looked good.

"We don't want to be late," I said. I still had to find Leslie and drop off my cookies.

"But wearing your shirt has changed my look. I need to adjust my hair."

This was nuts. The last thing Angelina needed to do was adjust the part of her that looked shiny, healthy, and normal.

"I'll meet you in class," she said.

What? What? What?

"No way!" I said. "It's my job to take you there."

Then her voice got stern. "If I can make it from Eagle River to Santa Fe, I can make it down the hallway to Mr. Guzman's class."

Wow. My cousin really lacked gratitude.

"Fine," I said. "I sit in the third row. There's an open desk two rows over. That one will probably be assigned to you."

I stormed out of the bathroom and hurried down the hallway. I felt really panicked. I knew I was wearing a lame shirt and that I could never take off this jacket. And I was already feeling a little hot. And I had to talk to a class captain dressed this way.

Luckily, I spotted Leslie talking to Robin and Derek outside the main office.

"I've got my cookies," I said. I took off my backpack and began unzipping it.

"Didn't you get my text?" Leslie asked. "We're making the cookie basket next week."

"Maybe you can freeze them," Derek said.

But I didn't know if that would work with dehydrated vegan cookies. So I didn't offer to do that. "That's okay. I'll just make more for next week."

"You're so easygoing," Leslie said.

"Totally," Robin added.

"Yeah," Derek said. "Why do you look stressed out?"

What a rude thing to say to me while I was panicking. I shrugged and looked at Derek as calmly as I could. "I just don't want to be late for class."

Derek smiled at me and reached in his pocket. "Here are some tardy slips. The office doesn't mind cutting the class captains some slack. We're responsible. They like us."

Even though it felt weird, I reached out and took the tardy slips. "Thanks."

"We'll look for you at lunch," Derek said.

I blinked at him before I ran off. I just didn't get it. First, why was he so nice to me? Second, why did it bug me *so much* that he was so nice to me?

Lucia and Rachel waved to me when I walked into

the classroom. I waved back. I caught Ava out of the corner of my eye when I sat down. "Where's Angelina?" she mouthed. I shrugged. I didn't have time to explain that she was in the bathroom adjusting her hair to match my cool bohemian tunic.

And then the bell rang and Angelina wasn't there. I took my seat and stared at the front board and hoped that I wouldn't get in any trouble. Mr. Guzman knew Angelina was coming; my mother had finalized all the arrangements last week. Angelina could just explain she'd gotten lost. And I'd play dumb. Being late on the first day wasn't too bad.

Please don't show up with freaky hair. Please don't show up with freaky hair.

I felt something land next to my arm. When I looked down, I saw Todd's hand jerking away. A note! I loved it when he sent me notes. I read it very quickly.

Why the jacket? Are you cold?

He was so sweet. He noticed that I was wearing a jacket in a warm room. I nodded, even though I could feel my head starting to sweat.

And then it happened. Something life-changing. Angelina bopped into my classroom. And I couldn't believe my eyes. She had *really* adjusted her hair. It was braided around her head. I couldn't tell if it looked cool or crazy. And it wasn't just braided with hair. There was something twisted in the braid. It was Ava's ribbon belt from her pajamas. Angelina had braided a belt to her head. What was wrong with her?

She and Mr. Guzman said a few things to each other, and then she turned around to face the class. My bohemian tunic! It had some weird symbol drawn on it. Was it an exclamation point? It was. No way. What made her think she could destroy my property? I would never do that. It was stunning. I mean, I left her alone looking normal, and five minutes later, she showed up to sixth grade wearing a punctuation mark and a crazy braid.

"This is our new class member," Mr. Guzman said.

I watched in horror as Angelina waved to my class. The only thing that made me feel better was that I knew this would only last a month.

"She's from Alaska and her name is Mint," Mr. Guzman said. "She's Lane Cisco's cousin. Lane, do you have anything to add to Mint's introduction?"

Why was my teacher calling Angelina by her middle name? Mint? Nobody called her that. Did they? My father's words flashed through my mind. "Protect her. She is your flesh and blood."

I cleared my throat. "My cousin is a very interesting person," I said. "Who is, um, really independent and (pause) creative and quick and knows cool stuff about bears."

There was total silence. But I think I could hear Ava's head exploding in disbelief. Angelina—er, uh—Mint waved again.

"She knows cool stuff about wolves too," Jagger said loudly.

"What fortunate news," Mr. Guzman says. "Because over the summer, our class read *Julie of the Wolves* by Jean Craighead George. I bet Mint will make an excellent resource for that."

I did not like the idea of *Mint* sharing information about wolves with my classmates in a group setting. Everybody would find out that she was super weird for sure! My mind kept zooming. She'd probably insist on wearing the wolf T-shirt to work on her presentation. And that would create a ton of group laughter. I imagined everybody laughing at her. Then I remembered that I was wearing that stupid shirt. Another note landed next to my hand. It was from Ava.

Did she braid my pajama belt to her head? Seriously.

I turned and gave Ava a quick nod.

"Lane," Mr. Guzman said. "Why don't you help Mint hand out our next geography assignment? We'll be mapping all the water resources in New Mexico."

"I love mapping!" Mint exclaimed.

I stood up on shaky knees and slowly walked to the front of the classroom. This jacket made me feel hotter and hotter and hotter. All I could think about was the sweat beads traveling down my back. I didn't like standing in front of people. *Walk. Walk. Walk.* When I got to the front of the room, some of my classmates' faces began to spin and I thought I might tip over. Wyatt Dover. Wren Ochoa. Paulette Feeley. Jagger. Lucia. Rachel— Then I felt an arm reach around my waist and steady me. Todd Romero? No, Angelina Mint Taravel. Then I watched as a blond blur hurried up to the front of the room. It was Ava.

She put her arm around me too and informed Mr. Guzman, "I'm taking Lane to the bathroom."

Ava didn't wait for permission as she pulled me out of the classroom and down the hallway. "Why are you wearing that lame jacket?"

We entered the bathroom and I didn't answer. Because I didn't want to admit that I was wearing a much lamer shirt underneath. But then Ava put two and two together. "You're wearing Angelina's weird clothes!"

I leaned against the bathroom wall. "Please don't judge me. I need water."

I felt Ava yank on my zipper. Then she released a horrendous gasp. "What's going on? You can't wear this in public."

She was right.

I tried to remember why I was wearing this shirt in the first place. "I was just trying to protect my cousin."

Ava scowled at me and then shook her head. "I'm going to Lost and Found to see if I can snag you a halfway decent shirt."

"No," I said. I couldn't let Ava do that. Wouldn't that be stealing? Letting my mom lie about Mint's permanent address to get her into the school for a month was dishonorable enough. I couldn't become a Lost and Found thief too. I'd signed an honor pledge. Forget whether the shirt would be scratchy or smell. What if the person who lost it recognized it and wanted it back? How would that look to my fellow class captains? I mean, they were planning to find me during lunch.

"Yes," Ava said. "No arguments. It's your only hope."

Ava sounded so certain that I decided she was probably right.

"I hope you realize what an evil swap your cousin just pulled," Ava said.

"No. No. No," I said. "This was my idea. I offered."

Ava's eyes grew very large. I'm sure that was surprising news. Because what sixth grader would ever offer to wear ridiculous clothes?

Ava stuck her pointer finger in my face. "She tricked you. That's what's going on, and that's what makes the swap evil. She's trying to ruin your reputation and destroy your relationship with Todd!"

Why did Ava think that? "No," I said. "She's not like that." My cousin wasn't crafty and mean. She was clueless and animal loving.

"Oh," Ava said before she walked out, "she's exactly like that. Trust me. I've got her number."

I kept leaning against the bathroom wall until Ava came back. Luckily, she returned with a cute, odorless green shirt that was made out of a super-soft fabric. We went into a stall and locked the door. I took off the jacket and the wolf shirt, and put the green one on.

"We're trashing this," Ava said, taking the wolf shirt and wadding it up into a ball.

"Um," I said. "That might upset my mom." Even though I was justified, my mom would never approve of me trashing my cousin's clothes.

"This shirt will reenter your life and haunt you if you don't destroy it right now," Ava said.

She was right. "Okay. But we have to keep her jacket."

Ava lifted my cousin's jacket by one finger and dangled it in front of me in disgust.

"That thing should have died in a garbage can years ago," Ava said.

"It's the only jacket she brought," I said.

"It goes against my better judgment, but fine," Ava said.

I felt so relieved. But when I reached for it, Ava didn't give it to me.

"Promise me you'll quit wearing it and hang it in the coat area," Ava said.

"Deal," I said.

When I walked back into the classroom wearing my semistolen, semiborrowed green shirt, my cousin was energetically placing the last geography assignment in front of Jagger. "I bet this would be harder if we lived in Alaska," he said. "I bet that state has a ton more water resources than ours."

She smiled hugely, and then said very loudly so the

whole class could hear her, "Yeah. Alaska's rivers, lakes, snowfields, wetlands, and glaciers make up about forty percent of the entire surface water for the United States. And in the spring, we get a bunch of ice jams."

"That's so interesting, Mint," Mr. Guzman said. "Ever since I was a kid, I've always wanted to visit Alaska."

Was I really going to have to call my cousin Mint? It sounded so weird when Mr. Guzman said it. Like a foreign word. Or the name of a pet rat. Mint? I said it several times in my head. *Mint. Mint. Mint.* Even though it seemed wrong on many levels, I guess this was what everybody was going to call her now. Even me.

I continued to half listen as *Mint* gushed about Alaskan ice jams. Was this how she flirted? Maybe it didn't matter whether Jagger thought she was cute. Because she came off as an annoying fact nerd. I went to my desk and sat down. After giving Jagger his assignment, my cousin knocked his desk with her hip, making a pencil roll onto the floor. Then she picked it up.

"I am *so* clumsy," she said, drumming the pencil against his desk. "Hey, are these your teeth marks?"

When she finally handed the pencil back to him, for the first time in my life, I saw Jagger Evenson blush.

"I'm not sure," Jagger said, holding the pencil with both hands, inspecting the pocked wood. "They could be."

Then I watched Mint reach into her pocket and pull out a pack of gum, which wasn't even allowed at my school. I looked to Mr. Guzman to see if he'd stop her. But he was sorting through a paper pile at his desk.

"Gum tastes way better," she said, tossing her hair over her shoulder.

Somehow the pajama belt had given her hair extra volume, making it look really good, especially when she tossed it.

Jagger blushed more.

It was disgusting! Angelina Mint Taravel *did* know how to flirt. Seeing this sent a chill down my spine. Cousin or not, I did not want her in my classroom. I wanted her *gone*.

· 10 ·

Even though Ava was my best friend, Rachel had become my favorite friend to call when things in my life were going lousy. Because she was a good listener. I'd dial her up and dump out all my anger, and she never interrupted me with her own problems. She was great like that. Especially when I found myself obsessing over the same rotten thing over and over.

"My pink bohemian shirt is totally ruined," I told Rachel. "I mean, this stain is as permanent as the Grand Canyon."

It might have been yesterday's news to my friends, but I could not stop staring at my grafittied top.

"It was rude of her to put an exclamation point on it," Rachel said. "Even if she thought it added style."

Who would think an exclamation mark added style? I just ignored that comment.

"Mint is in the kitchen right now with my mom helping her make dinner," I said. "She is so irritating."

As the days ticked by, I found Mint difficult to be around even when I wasn't around her. She was powerfully annoying. Every little thing she did got under my skin: The way she wrote in her journal at night. The way she stole my parents' attention and talked to them as if they were her good friends. The way she sat at her desk and raised her hand and answered questions as if she belonged there, when her *real school* address was in Alaska. The way she took off her socks and left them on my bedroom floor in little sock wads. It was rough.

"Maybe you should go watch television," Rachel said. "Take your mind off her."

"I think I should tell my mom what Mint did," I said. I kept rubbing my finger across the black mark. It felt like a different texture than the rest of my shirt. It felt like a different texture than anything I'd ever touched.

"Wouldn't you have to tell your mom that you threw her wolf shirt in the garbage?" Rachel asked.

She was right. Instead of looking like a person who had an inconsiderate cousin who destroyed my clothes, I ran the risk of looking like the inconsiderate person who threw my cousin's clothes away. My situation felt so unfair.

"Do you want to talk about something else?" Rachel asked. "When are we going to buy tickets for Ava's concert?"

Ava's *Sleeping Beauty* concert was still weeks away. Because we were supportive friends, we tried to attend all of them. Sometimes I wished Ava played the guitar or ukulele instead of the cello. Symphonies could be boring. Not only did Ava usually have a small part, she was mostly hidden behind her cello. This time Ava had assured us that she would be playing her cello during most of the songs. And when she wasn't playing, she promised us she would try to lean to the left so that we could see her better.

"Has she showed you her callus?" Rachel asked. "It's huge. She's practicing like crazy."

"No, she hasn't. Let's not worry about her concert yet. Can I vent more about Mint?" I asked. Because that was the whole reason I'd called Rachel. It's like she'd forgotten what a great listener she used to be.

"Sure. Do you mind if I draw squids while you talk?"

"Go ahead," I said.

Knock. Knock. Knock.

"Great," I huffed. "I think my least favorite houseguest ever just knocked on my door."

"At least she knocked," Rachel offered. "You are sharing the room."

When my mom poked her head in my room, I felt a little relieved.

"Honey, Mint and I have decided to run to the store," she asked. "Do you want to come?"

It really bugged me that my mom was calling my cousin "Mint." I thought that was going to be something that would only happen at school.

"I'll stay here," I said. "Can you get more cereal?" I hated it when the box became overly crumb-filled at the bottom. All those little particles made the milk soupy.

Mint barreled into my room and raced toward her duffel bag. "Let me grab my wallet."

I thought it was weird that Mint thought she had to buy her own food at the grocery store. Didn't she know my parents had that covered?

"Consider it an early birthday present," my mom said.

"You are such a cool aunt!" Mint cheered, wrapping her arms around my mom.

"Why aren't you talking to me anymore?" Rachel asked.

"Something is happening in my bedroom," I explained. "I think my mom is taking Mint clothes shopping."

"Maybe she can buy you a replacement shirt!" Rachel suggested.

But if that happened, I thought I also might have to buy Mint a replacement wolf shirt and I would rather get attacked by a pack of cats than do that.

"I know exactly where I want to go!" Mint said. "It's the hippest shop in Santa Fe."

I stared at Mint in disbelief. How would she know where the hippest store was?

"Skull Coast!" Mint cheered.

I almost dropped the phone. "Mint wants to go to Skull Coast to buy clothes," I told Rachel in a horrified and stunned voice.

"The thrasher store with the giant spiders?" Rachel asked.

How did Mint already know the creepiest place to shop in Santa Fe? Supposedly, that place kept tarantulas inside plastic boxes throughout the store. Didn't Mint have any impulses toward normal stuff?

"I don't think we've ever shopped there," my mom said. "Have we?"

"Rachel," I said. "I've got to go." There was no way I could send my mom and Mint to that place without my guidance. As much as I wanted to stay and talk to Rachel, I needed to make sure nothing insane happened.

As soon as my mom parked the car, I got a phone call from Ava. But I didn't answer it. I stayed focus on my task. No insane things could happen.

"Wow," my mom said as we walked through the glass front doors. "They sure have a lot of black apparel."

This was an understatement. Skull Coast had zero variety. The T-shirts were black. The pants were black. The shorts were black. And they didn't have a girl's section. It was a total dude store.

"How did you hear about this place?" my mom asked as she walked past a metal pole showcasing a T-shirt that said I POOPED TODAY.

"A guy who sits near me mentioned it," Mint said.

"Who?" I asked. Because I couldn't think of a single person in my class who would enter this store.

"Tuma," Mint said.

I felt sick to my stomach. Why was Mint talking to Tuma? He was trouble.

"Is that a tarantula?" my mom asked, lifting a shaky

finger toward a Plexiglas box holding the biggest fanged spider I'd ever seen.

My life didn't even feel like my life. A week ago I never even knew where this strip mall was located, now I was standing inside its weirdest store next to a giant, hairy spider.

A pimply teenager with three lip rings approached us. "If you've got any questions, shoot them my way."

"Where are your Damaged Earth shirts?" Mint asked.

"Back corner," the teenager said. "Buy one, get one fifty percent off."

"Cool!" Mint cheered.

My mom and I followed Mint to the back corner. And as if things couldn't get any worse, I actually spotted Tuma in the store. Which was doubly tragic. Because it meant that Tuma would eventually spot me.

"You came," Tuma said.

I watched as he approached my cousin. I couldn't believe that she'd convinced my mom to drive her to this store. Was she planning to hang out with him? Did she like him? Did she *like* like him?

"This feels so wrong," I told my mom as we stood back and let Tuma and Mint chat while they looked through a pile of T-shirts.

"Come here," my mom said, pulling me behind a round rack of black jeans.

"She had a disappointing phone call with Aunt Betina the other day and I'm trying to cheer her up," my mom said.

"We are in a store filled with tarantulas, gross clothes,

and a lame kid rumored to have a violent streak from my school," I snapped.

"Why are you making this harder than it needs to be?" my mom asked. "She's making a friend."

A friend? Mint flipped her hair several times while she and Tuma held up various T-shirts. I couldn't believe it. Did Mint seriously like Tuma? The one positive outcome of Mint possibly *like* liking Tuma was that she'd stop flirting with Jagger.

"Mom, I am not making anything harder," I said.

The sound of Tuma and Mint laughing interrupted our fight.

"Totally get that one," Tuma said.

"Aunt Claire?" Mint called. "I think I found my shirts."

I rolled my eyes. I couldn't even imagine what Mint had found that she thought was wearable.

"Those are nice," my mom said, as the cashier rang up our purchase.

It turns out I was wrong about everything being black in the store. Mint had found a tight-fitting, dark green T-shirt with a bunch of smeared patches of red on it. If you stood back far enough, the green spaces formed a world globe. And she also picked out a shirt that had a camouflage pattern on it that said DON'T SHOOT. It surprised me that these shirts even existed, let alone that I would be related to somebody who wanted to wear them to middle school.

While I stood beside my mom at the register, I could feel Tuma approaching me. I didn't turn my head.

"So what's Ava doing tonight?" Tuma asked me.

It creeped me out that Tuma asked me something so personal about Ava. They weren't friends. And I was pretty sure she wouldn't want me to discuss what she was doing. "She's chillin'," I said, trying to sound as nonchalant as possible.

"When's her next cello thing?" he asked.

I glanced at Mint and shot her daggers. If it weren't for her, I wouldn't be in this awkward situation. I would be at home talking to Rachel on the phone.

"Next month," I said. And then I turned my body away so he knew I was finished talking to him.

"Ready?" my mom asked as she finished signing the store's receipt.

"Yeah," I said.

As we climbed into the car and started driving home, I kept feeling a weird tingling sensation on my arms. Like maybe a spider was crawling on them. But every time I looked down they were fine.

"Tuma told me that the class captains get to plan all the school parties for the year," Mint said.

This meant Mint and Tuma had been talking about me. I didn't approve of that at all.

"Your school always has the best themes," my mom said in an upbeat voice. "Last year they had a luau."

I actually didn't think the luau was very fun. The music felt too goofy and it didn't make you want to dance. Our class was going to love our disco theme. When I closed my eyes, I could imagine everybody in my class dancing their butts off. Too bad I couldn't tell anybody about our disco theme yet.

"Theme parties bum me out," Mint said.

"Why?" my mom asked as we turned down a road lined with aging, mud-colored, stucco homes.

"Because you don't get to be yourself. You have to pretend to be a totally different person."

"Good point," my mom said, giving me a quick smile.

"I totally disagree," I said. "I think theme parties are awesome. They give you the chance to be yourself and wear interesting costumes. And this year we have the best theme ever."

"Ooh. What is it?" Mint asked.

I wasn't even tempted to break my allegiance to my class captains and tell her. "We don't tell anybody until we make the official announcement at school."

"Ooh. I hope I'm around long enough to find out what it is," Mint said.

"Yeah," I mumbled. But that wasn't how I felt at all.

· 11 ·

Mint may have driven me nuts, but she drove Ava totally bonkers. One day, out of the blue, she started sending me text messages about how to get rid of her.

> Ava: Go on a hunger strike until your parents send her back.
> Ava: Lucia and Rachel and I will join you on the hunger strike.
> Ava: Poison her.
> Ava: Put her into contact with people who have the flu until she gets it.
> Ava: Or find somebody with chicken pox! Does Javier still have them?
> Ava: Turn your back on her! Save yourself!

I never knew how to respond to these texts. It felt as if Ava wasn't joking around.

Mint's arrival also put a real strain on my relationship with Todd. Because even though Ava had clearly explained girl code to Mint at our pj party, Mint was terrible at remembering it. Especially the part about hijacking boys. She talked to Jagger *and* Todd like they were long lost friends every day before class started.

> Day Two: Hi, Jagger. Nice shoes. I bet you're a super fast runner.
>
> Day Three: Hi, Todd. Did I ever tell you about a fishing captain I knew whose last name was Romero? He was a local hero. Until he get lost at sea. The Bering Strait is *so* dangerous.
>
> Day Four: Jagger! Do you need more gum?

And then came the worst of it. During the fifth day of her stay with us, I learned the truth about how close Mint was getting with Jagger and Todd. Because Ava texted me all about it.

I was not prepared for this text at all. I was getting ready to go out to dinner to a fancy restaurant to celebrate Mint's first week of school.

Ava: Do you know that Mint texted Todd and Jagger a photo of Alaska?

I could hardly believe what my phone was telling me. I just stared at it. Why would Todd and Jagger want Mint to text them a photo of Alaska? I didn't even have pants on yet. I was still picking out which pair to wear. But clothes could come later. I had to text Ava back.

Me: NO FREAKING WAY! HOW DID SHE GET TODD'S NUMBER?
Ava: You should ask her. Then forbid her from texting Todd. And Jagger. He's my crush. Mine. GIRL CODE!!
Me: Are you sure she's texting Jagger?
Ava: Like a machine. 4 times yesterday.
Me: How do you know this?
Ava: I sneaked a look at Jagger's phone.
Me: You need to stop doing that!

Because Jagger and Ava sometimes walked to school with a group of seventh graders, Ava would make an excuse to borrow his phone and then glance at his history.

Ava: I'm learning important stuff. Don't judge!
Me: Sorry. Just worried.

Knock. Knock. Knock.
I jumped a little and dropped my phone.
"Lane? Are you ready for dinner?" my mom asked. "We have six o'clock reservations."
This was ridiculous. First, I still hadn't put on pants. Second, we never went anyplace that required reservations. Why did we have to celebrate Mint's first week of school? It sucked.

I chose a pair of black pants that flared at the bottom. Ava thought they looked like cowgirl pants, but I didn't think she had seen enough cowgirls to make that assessment. "Where is Mint?" I asked. She'd asked to be dropped off at my dad's work after school. But she couldn't have stayed there all day. That would bore a person my age to death.

"She's still with your father," my mom said. "She really hit it off with his co-workers. They're teaching her how to prune."

Why did she want to become friends with my dad's co-workers? Yuck. Mint was becoming more like bacteria every day. Spreading. Spreading. Spreading.

As my mom and I drove to the restaurant, I thought it might be a good time to complain about my cousin and get a little sympathy.

"I cannot wait for her to return to Alaska," I said.

My mother groaned. "Don't say that. You don't mean it."

I stared at her. "I absolutely mean it. She's weird. And she makes my life difficult."

"She is a good person," my mother said.

It was amazing that in just a few days my cousin had figured out a way to poison my family's minds. Why did they like her so much? She was a total mess. "You're only saying nice things about her because you don't have to go to school with her," I said.

My mother pulled into the restaurant parking lot. "That's not true. I like my niece. She's spunky. And I've talked to Mr. Guzman and he says that Mint is getting along fabulously with everybody at the school. He said he's never seen anything like it before."

Whoa. My mom was talking to Mr. Guzman about Mint? She shouldn't be doing that. Mint was temporary. We needed to treat her like an exchange student who we sort of hoped we'd never see again. Unless we happened to travel to Alaska. Which, based on what she'd shared with me about their bear population, I hoped we never did.

"Well, Mr. Guzman is wrong. She doesn't get along with *everybody*," I said. And I thought about telling her how Mint's behavior made Ava, Lucia, and Rachel, and me basically want to vomit. But I didn't say that. I thought of something to say that my mother could not disagree with.

"Showing up to a new school and changing your name to an ice cream flavor is lame."

My mother turned off the engine. Then she looked at me with a stern expression. "When I was in college, my first semester, I told people that my name was Clarice."

"Is your name Clarice?" I asked. I'd only ever heard people call her Claire.

"No. Changing my name was a fun thing to do. I understand where Mint's coming from. She's exploring her identity. So stop judging her."

I blinked several times. I just couldn't relate. Because I liked my identity. So changing your name didn't seem like a fun thing to do at all.

"Clarice is a better fake name than Mint," I said, trying to stop the fight. Really, I didn't want to start an argument with my mom. I just wanted her to understand where I was coming from.

"It's her middle name," my mom said with a frustrated tone. "Lots of people decide to go by their middle names. And she didn't pick the name Mint. My sister did."

I nodded. Because she had a point.

When we walked inside the restaurant, I spotted Mint right away, because she was wearing a plastic bib with a picture of a big orange crab on it.

As we approached the table, she waved furiously at us. It annoyed me for several reasons. The biggest being that my mother returned her wave. With a lot of enthusiasm.

"They let you pick out your own crab," Mint said, jerking her thumb toward a fish tank.

I did not plan to murder a crab for my dinner. And I said that. "I'm not killing an animal for my meal."

Mint tilted her head. "Are you eating only salad?"

My mom laughed at this and sat down in her chair. "Crustaceans aren't for everyone."

But this sort of bothered me. Because it made Mint sound more mature than me. And she wasn't. On her first day of school she braided her hair with a pajama belt!

"I think I might get the crab too," my dad said.

"I feel like splurging tonight as well," my mom said, picking up her menu.

I was stunned. Everybody at my table was going to kill a crab. At first, I was disgusted. But then I felt left out.

"What do they come with?" I asked.

"You get your choice of three sides," Mint gushed. "I'm

getting papaya salad, garlic noodles, and braised string beans."

I felt caught off guard. I didn't really want to eat those things, but suddenly dinner felt very competitive.

"What a fantastic selection," my dad said. "But I bet the portions are enormous. I don't think I can tuck away a whole crab. Would you like to split?" He reached across the table and touched my mom's hand.

"Of course," my mom said to him, placing her other hand on top of his.

Then everybody looked at me. I couldn't believe it. Did my parents expect me to split a crab dinner with Angelina Mint Taravel? This. Was. Not. Happening.

"You don't have to split," my mom said. "I know you don't want to pick out a crab for dinner."

The way my mother said this made me feel like a complete child. I mean, it was like the whole table thought I was a baby. I was twelve. I should have been able to pick out my own crab. So I stood up and stated that very clearly.

"I can select my own crab," I said. "If everybody else is eating crab, then I want to eat crab too."

My dad frowned at me sympathetically. "You don't have to do that."

"I want to do that," I said.

"You're not picking out your own crab," my mom reminded me. "You're picking out one to share."

"I know. I don't mind sharing a dinner," I lied. "But I want to be the crab picker," I explained, pointing to myself. My stomach tightened at the thought of selecting which crab would die. But I couldn't back down in front of Mint. I had to show my parents that she wasn't *that* special. "Mint, let's go to the tank."

And she stood up and grabbed my arm in a hugging way (that annoyed me) and off we went to select our crab.

Standing in front of the tank, watching all these orangey claws reach toward the glass begging for freedom was tough to take.

"You look totally sad," Mint said.

And I couldn't hold in my frustration any longer.

"Ava says you texted Todd," I told her.

Mint put her arm around me, and gave me a strong squeeze. It made me want to puke.

"Well," she said, "he texted me first."

I almost fell into the crab tank's glass wall. That was impossible. There was no way Todd texted Mint first.

"When did he text you?" I didn't believe a word of it.

"Two days ago," she said. "He was asking me a question about Jagger."

This was terrible. Did Jagger *really* like Mint? *Really?* Jagger was cool and funny and interested in Ava.

"Well, you can't like Jagger," I said. "He's Ava's."

Mint shook her head slowly. "Nobody told me that. How was I supposed to know?"

I thought back to the trampoline party. Ava had tried to keep that a secret. But it was sort of obvious. At least to people with normal social intelligence.

"Wait a minute," I said. "I thought you liked Tuma."

Mint's eyes grew wide with surprise. "Did he tell you that?"

"No," I said. "I don't talk to Tuma. But you met up with him at Skull Coast and picked out shirts together."

"I like his style," Mint said. "But I do not like Tuma. I've already given him the friendship talk. And we've both agreed that we don't want to be anything more."

"What?" I asked. She'd been at my school for one week and she'd already managed to have a friendship talk with a guy? She was out of control. I needed to start laying down some boundaries.

"I don't want you to text Todd anymore," I said. "It's a girl code violation."

"Really?" Mint asked. "Because he says the nicest things about you."

This blew my mind. Todd Romero was texting nice things about me to my weird cousin?

"Show me your phone!" I said. "What did he say?"

She shook her head again. It was so annoying when she shook her head. "I left my phone in your dad's car. I thought it would be rude to bring it to the restaurant."

How lame was she? Todd was texting her about me and she doesn't tell me.

"Don't you want to pick out a crab?" Mint asked.

I focused on the tank. The crabs crawled around looking so pathetic. I lifted my finger to the glass and pointed at a doomed crab's face.

"They can tell what's about to happen. Their eyes are filled with fear," I said.

Mint pointed at the exact same crab. "That's its butt," she said.

My cousin was so annoying.

"Fine. You pick it out," I said. I didn't care if we get the one with the scared butt or not. I power walked back to the table and sat down.

"You don't have to eat a crab," my mother said, leaning over and patting my arm. "You can get chicken teriyaki. Or a hamburger. Or I bet they have a grilled cheese sandwich on the kids' menu."

Yeah, right. I was *not* going to eat a grilled cheese sandwich off the kids' menu while Angelina Mint Taravel ate our crab. Never! I could eat half that stinking crab.

Conversation was okay at first, but then it turned rotten. Mint started making demands.

"Lane, I've been wondering if I could borrow one of your dresser drawers," she asked. "You can pick which one."

Why would she wait to mention this in front of my parents? She'd ambushed me. Did she want my parents to think I was some sort of drawer hoarder incapable of sharing? Because I wasn't. It just never occurred to me that Mint would need to unpack her duffel bag. She seemed to enjoy keeping all her belongings hidden inside it.

"Of course Lane doesn't mind," my mother said, speaking for me.

"You should take two drawers," my dad said. I shot him a look. Was he kidding?

"Good idea," my mom said. "One for socks. One for your bras and underwear."

"Mom!" I said. Why did she need to say that in public—and in front of my dad?

"Is that okay, Lane?" Mint asked, blinking at me in a kind way.

"Sure," I said. "I can clean a drawer out tonight." I tried to pretend that my dad hadn't said two.

"But I think two drawers would be better," my mom encouraged. "Give your cousin a little room."

Wow. My mother's logic was totally messed up. It would be better for Mint to have more room. Didn't she see that meant I'd have less room?

"You are such a trouper," my dad said.

"I really appreciate all your help," Mint said. "You're awesome."

I watched her grab a dinner roll from the basket and split it open with her thumbs. Then I felt a hand on me and I jumped a little. But it was my mom.

"You really are awesome," she said in a sappy way.

Gag. What would my cousin ask for next?

"So are you learning anything interesting at school yet?" my dad asked.

Mint nodded enthusiastically. "I have learned a ton about New Mexico."

Then she listed the most random facts about my state. She made it sound really weird. Which it wasn't.

Santa Fe is the highest capital city in the United States.
In October, Las Cruces makes the world's largest
    enchilada.

Hundreds of thousands of bats live in the Carlsbad
   Caverns.
The first atomic bombs were developed and tested in
   New Mexico.
An extraterrestrial spacecraft with aliens may have
   crashed in Roswell.

"You've got a mind for facts," my father said.

"Well, I want to remember all this stuff so I can tell my
mom about it. I think she'd really like it here," Mint said.

I didn't like the way that sounded.

"You mean like when she visits?" I asked, hoping the
answer would be immediate.

Mint sat straight up and grinned. "Yeah, but wouldn't it
be great if she came and fell in love with it and we moved
here?"

The room spun a little.

"That would be great!" my mom said. "It would be so
much fun having you and Betina around."

"And Clark," my dad said. "Let's not forget anybody."

"Right," Mint said, letting her grin fade.

I decided not to freak out at the table, because I figured
the odds of Mint and her mom and new stepdad relocating
were low.

When our crab arrived, I wished I had been staring at
a hamburger.

"Just accept that this is going to be pretty messy experience," my dad said, tying the ends of his bib together.

"Here you go," Mint said, handing me what looked like

a pair of pliers. "Are there any parts you're craving? A particular leg or claw?"

This poor animal looked so dead. And the chef had arranged the condiments so our crustacean appeared to be clutching a ramekin filled with pink sauce.

"I'm going to start with our beans," I said.

The sound of people cracking open a crab was very unsettling. Also, crab juice squirts very far.

"This is delicious!" Mint said. "In Alaska, I feel like I'm always eating salmon in the fall. Crab is a nice change."

"I wish we had that problem," my dad said with a chuckle.

"We should buy tickets and go," my mom said. "Every year I think about visiting."

"Ooh," Mint said. "Do it!"

That was when I swallowed wrong and began choking on a bean. My mom gently slapped my back. As quick as I could, I grabbed my water to try to wash it down.

"No," I said. "Not Alaska."

"But you've never been," my dad said. "I bet you'd love it. They have moose there."

Cough. Cough. "Hawaii," I gasped. "I'd rather go to Hawaii."

My mom stopped patting my back.

"I'll show you how to lick a glacier," Mint said.

"That's disgusting," I said. *Cough. Cough.* "I just lost my appetite."

With that, I pushed away my beans. And then I stuck my tongue out at our poor, dead crab. And just when I thought things couldn't get any worse, something really bizarre happened. I heard a cell phone ring and it was Mint's. I was really surprised to hear this. Because she'd said she'd left her cell phone in my dad's car. Why was she lying to me about that? What else was she lying to me about? I couldn't stop glaring at her.

"It's my mom!" she said, cheerfully placing her phone next to her head. "She said she'd phone me as soon as the ship got to their port in Italy."

I turned to my mom. "Shouldn't she take that call in the lobby?" My mom couldn't stand it when people talked on their cell phones at the table.

My mom motioned to Mint. "Follow me up front."

Mint and my mom weaved their way around people's tables and turned a corner, out of view. I was just about to tell my dad that I could not stand Mint when his phone started to buzz.

"I need to take this," he said, getting up.

Sitting alone at the table with two dead crabs wasn't ideal. Because, in addition to looking like dead crabs, they smelled like dead crabs. So I just decided to breathe half as much as normal and stare at the saltshaker until my family returned. But then something unexpected happened. I felt a person tap me on the shoulder. And when I turned around I was shocked to see Todd.

"Hi, Lane," Todd said.

I felt my face blush. He looked very dressed up in khaki pants and a cute sweater. Why was he here?

"I didn't know you came to this restaurant," he said. "My family is celebrating my grandparents' anniversary."

I blinked at him in disbelief.

"We're over there," he said.

I followed the aim of his finger to a crowded table filled with the remains of a big white cake.

"I brought you a piece," he said, handing me a small dish loaded with a slice of heavily frosted cake.

"Thank you," I said.

"I've been trying to get your attention all night," he said.

My heart raced very quickly when I heard this. I loved the idea of Todd trying to get my attention all night.

"I've got to get back to my table now," he said. Then he did something terrible. He handed me a second piece of cake.

"Oh, thanks," I said. But I didn't think I could eat two pieces of cake.

"It's for Mint," he said. "Does she eat cake?"

I didn't even answer that question, because I didn't even care.

"Thanks," I said. "You'd better go. My dad is coming back."

"He can know that we're friends, can't he?" Todd asked.

But if he knew we were friends, he might eventually suspect that we were more than friends. Which we most definitely were. We passed each other notes all the time. And we'd held hands. Twice.

1) Before lunch two weeks ago.

2) After lunch one week ago.

"He's taking an important business call," I said. "Next time?"

"Okay," Todd said. "I'll text you later."

"Cool," I said. Then I waved.

And as soon as Todd left, I inhaled Mint's piece of cake. There was no way I was going to let Todd give my crazy cousin a slice of his grandparents' anniversary cake. No. Way. But then I realized that I didn't want to have to explain who had brought me my own piece of cake. So I ate that one too. And then I stashed the empty plates on a nearby table whose occupants had just left. By the time my parents got back, I was feeling very full and extremely energized.

"My mom is having an amazing honeymoon," Mint said. "She and Clark just visited the Colosseum."

Gag. I'd heard of the Colosseum in fourth grade. It was a place where crowds gathered to watch gladiators fight vicious animals to the death, like tigers, elephants, lions, bears, and ostriches. What a rotten place to visit on your honeymoon.

"Aren't you going to eat more crab?" my mom asked, pointing to the big orange shell on the platter that I had not touched.

"I'm good," I said. I turned around and sneaked another look at Todd. And when I did that, I realized that Mint had had him in clear view the entire evening. Not only had she lied to me about her cell phone. She knew Todd was in the restaurant and she hadn't told me.

I turned back to the table and watched Mint as she cracked open our crab's larger claw. Using a small fork, she dug out chunks of glistening white meat from its shell. I watched her place it in her tiny mouth. Then she cracked another shell. And something about the way she pried open and devoured that crustacean, little bite by little bite, made me realize that even though Angelina Mint Taravel was my own flesh and blood, I shouldn't trust her.

· 12 ·

I had three more weeks left with Angelina Mint Taravel.
How much more terrible could things get?

So much more terrible!

"I am going to try something new with my hair," Mint
said as we were getting ready to leave for school.

She was wearing her camouflage T-shirt that said
DON'T SHOOT for a third time and it was pointless to try and
stop her.

I went to the kitchen and lifted my Tupperware container filled with vegan lemon-poppy-seed cookies into
my backpack. Though I'd never admit it to her face, Mint
was right when she accused my dehydrated chocolate chip
cookies of looking like dog turds. I felt lucky to have a second chance to make something better for the cookie basket.

After I zipped my backpack, Mint came out of the

bathroom with eight jumbo straws pieced through a loose bun on her head. She looked ridiculous.

"I saw them at the store yesterday by the fountain drinks," she said. "The clerk let me have them for free."

Didn't they have convenience stories in Alaska? Didn't she know the straws were always free? That normal people didn't style their hair with them?

"I am going to be totally honest," I said. "That is not your best look."

Mint frowned at me. "You are *so* conservative."

What? My cousin was really pushing my buttons. I wasn't conservative. I was ambitious. And I had a whole container of vegan cookies to prove it.

"Listen. Do you want my advice or not?" I asked her. I folded my arms across my chest and stared at her with my serious face.

She shook her head. "Not really. You want me to do things your way. But I do stuff a different way."

Wow. What was she saying? I did stuff the way you were supposed to do stuff in order to live a fantastic life. Didn't she see that? Couldn't she see how great I was at making awesome friends like Ava and Rachel and Lucia? Plus, I'd won class captain. It was insulting. She should have been thankful I was trying to help her. "Fine," I said. "Wear straws on your head. I don't care."

I considered the conversation we'd had in front of my closet a fight. And after our fight, I did not want to talk to Mint. But she kept trying to talk to me. All the way to school I answered her in short, huffy sentences.

OUR DRIVEWAY CONVERSATION
WAITING FOR THE BUS

"Do you think we'll still be working on mapping New Mexico's water resources today?" Mint asked.

"Probably."

"Cool. I reviewed all my notes last night."

Sigh.

OUR BUS CONVERSATION

"Wow. Don't you think the bus smells like burned peanuts this morning?" Mint commented.

I inhaled a bunch of bus air and shook my head. I just smelled my awesome cookies.

OUR PRE-CLASS HALLWAY CONVERSATION

"Paulette Feeley is wearing the cutest boots. I want to ask her where she got them."

Double sigh. "They're hideous."

I said this because Paulette was wearing the grossest boots I'd ever seen. They looked like they were covered in horse crap or pig crap or worse.

Then I overheard one of the worst conversations of my life. Seriously. It made me want to die.

"Hey! Is that a *Dwarf Massacre Three: Axe of Doom* comic book?" Mint asked.

I turned my head a little and glanced at Jagger's magazine. It looked pretty violent.

"You know about *Dwarf Massacre Three?*" Jagger asked.

"I just barely won that game. I was stuck in the slime caves below the pirate ship forever before I found the way out," Mint said.

I couldn't believe that Mint played that game.

"Todd and I are stuck in the slimes cave right now," Jagger said. "Every time I think we're getting out, the monsters keep respawning."

"Yeah. You need to kill them quicker," Mint said.

"We're trying," Jagger said, sounding exhausted. "So, is there a way out of the slime caves or do we need to go back?"

"How much do you want me to reveal about the secret rock?" Mint asked, flipping her hair over her shoulder.

"Everything!" Jagger said.

INSIDE MY OWN HEAD CONVERSATION
Ava is going to die when I tell her about this.

A note landed next to my arm. It was from Ava.

We pick groups for that Julie wolf book today. Me, you, Jagger, Todd. Okay?

I turned back to Ava and nodded. I hoped Lucia and Rachel didn't feel left out. And I hoped Jagger didn't want to be grouped with Mint. Did my cousin know she was ruining everybody's lives?

Mint plopped down in the seat behind me and leaned forward. "Paulette says she got her boots in Texas."

I didn't respond. "She has an aunt who's a rodeo star and lives in Amarillo," Mint went on. "Apparently she can hog-tie almost anything in under a minute."

I still didn't respond. *But Mint kept gabbing.*

"One of my mom's favorite songs is about Amarillo. It's about a divorced rodeo guy who's trying to drive from San Antonio to Amarillo by morning so he can get bucked by the number eight bull."

This was insane. What was wrong with my cousin? I didn't care about songs about divorced men getting bucked by bulls in Texas. I flipped around. "You talk too much!"

She pulled away and sat back in her seat. "I don't know if that's true. I think I'm just more social than you are."

I felt anger crawling through me. How dare she say something awful about me. I was plenty social!

"You are acting like a dweeb," I snapped.

Ava only sat a row away, but she heard me say this and she smiled. Which made me feel good for one second. But then I worried that other people might have heard me and I felt bad. I thought about what my dad had said about protecting my flesh and blood, which I definitely was not doing by calling my cousin a dweeb in front of my entire class.

"I didn't mean to snap at you," I mumbled. But Mint

never said anything back. So I didn't know if she was pouting. Or maybe she never heard my apology.

I watched as everybody hurried to sit down right as the last bell rang. I used to flitter around before the bell rang too. I'd go talk to Lucia or Rachel or Todd or peek inside the tank that held our class frogs. But ever since Mint had arrived, I hadn't felt like it. I'd felt burdened and pretty worried. I thought about turning around and apologizing more loudly, but I also didn't feel like doing that at all. So I didn't.

Before I could stew much more in my own problems, I was ripped to attention. Derek was standing in the doorway, waving at me. I waved back. And then he entered my classroom.

"Can I talk to Lane?" Derek asked. "It's about our class-captain meeting."

"Sure," Mr. Guzman said. "Lane, I'll give you five minutes."

It was a pleasant feeling knowing everybody was watching me as I walked out of the classroom into the hallway. I wondered what Derek needed to tell me. It must have been super important. We stood by my classroom next to a row of lockers.

"Did you forget?" he asked.

I didn't know what Derek was talking about. What was I supposed to remember?

"The vegan cookies," Derek said. "For the cookie basket. Everybody gave theirs to Leslie before school."

"I didn't forget!" I said. "They're in my backpack."

Derek smiled and put his arm on my shoulder. "Cool. I'll tell Leslie. Give them to her at lunch. She was freaking out about it."

"I made Leslie freak out?" I asked, pointing to myself.

"It wasn't just you. Fiona's cookies look like crap. She overbaked them. I don't think it's a huge deal," Derek said with a shrug. "But both Leslie and Robin can go mental over small details."

"Oh," I said. It suddenly felt as if Derek and I were dissing the other class captains in the hallway, and I'd rather not be doing that. "My cookies look pretty good. I mean, they're vegan. So they look a little different."

"Don't sweat it," he said. "I'll find you at lunch."

"Yeah," I said. "That sounds cool." But that wasn't the total truth, because I was really looking forward to just hanging out with my friends.

When I walked back into the classroom, everybody sat quietly focused, listening to Mr. Guzman.

"You all look wonderful and well rested," Mr. Guzman said. "And ready to hear some news about our next class assignment."

A couple of people groaned. It sounded like Morgan Dover and Thad Cartwright. Typically, they were known for groaning because they were the least excited about learning. I slipped into my seat and glanced back at Ava. She was very good at predicting news. I think it came from her tendencies to snoop and eavesdrop and guess well.

"It's time to pick your groups for *Julie of the Wolves*."

Two more people groaned. But the rest of us were pretty jazzed. Because group assignments meant group time. And that basically meant talking with your friends for an hour each day.

"Are you curious to know what you'll be doing?" Mr. Guzman asked.

Of course we were curious. It was our first group assignment of the year.

"You'll all be doing a transformational genre exercise," Mr. Guzman said.

Excited? I turned back and frowned at Ava. Because a transformational genre exercise sounded hard.

"What it means is that you're each going to take a section of the novel and transform it into a different genre."

"Like a movie!" Paulette asked. "Will we film each other?"

That seemed unlikely. Our school had a policy against filming students on school property. I flipped back to Ava and watched her roll her eyes. I really enjoyed it when Ava made rude facial expressions aimed at people I didn't totally like.

"No, not a movie," Mr. Guzman said. "We're going to transform sections of the novel into a play. You'll each be assigned a different section. And at the end, we'll have a play of the entire book."

A note landed next to my arm. It was from Todd.

I hope we get in the same group.

I wrote at the bottom of the note in big letters so he could read them.

ME TOO :)

Glancing around the room, I caught Rachel looking at me. She pointed to herself and then pointed to me. Uh-oh. Mr. Guzman said all groups were made of four or less. There wasn't any room for Rachel to join our group. So I shrugged. I'd explain later. And maybe buy her a candy bar to smooth things over. I'd appeal to her sweet tooth.

"Now I have some fun news," Mr. Guzman said.

I hoped that it was going to be amazingly fun information such as making awesome costumes using glitter or feathers using hot glue guns.

"Instead of assigning groups, I thought we could shake things up."

That didn't make any sense. Mr. Guzman never shook things up. I watched as my teacher pulled a tweed hat out of his desk drawer.

"Inside this hat are the names of every student in the room. We're going to be divided into seven groups of four. Listen for your name."

This was insane. We should get to pick our groups. How else would we be guaranteed to work with our friends?

"Fun idea," Paulette said.

I did some more glaring at the back of her head.

"Actually," Mr. Guzman said, "Mint suggested it. And it did seem like a fun idea."

I looked at Mint. She smiled big. I wanted to choke her.

After Mr. Guzman called our names, he asked us to walk to the front of the classroom and write our name on the board underneath our group number.

"Group one," Mr. Guzman said. "Jasmine, Lexy, Thad, and Lucia."

Poor Lucia. Thad wouldn't do any work. And Lexy always smelled like a pork chop and had a runny nose. Jasmine would probably be okay.

"Group two," Mr. Guzman said. "Wren, Wyatt, Coral, and Isaac."

Other than Coral, I didn't have terribly strong opinions about anybody in that group, but based on how they dressed, they were some of the more creative people in my class.

"Group three," he announced. "Rachel, Kevin, Felipe, and Lane."

Oh no! I was Lane. And I didn't hear Todd's name in my group.

"Group four," he said. "Paulette, Tuma, Bobby, and Ava."

I turned and looked at Ava. No. Way. This was unbelievably lame. I mean, it was sort of evil.

"Group five," Mr. Guzman said. "Todd, Jagger, Kimmie, and Mint."

This was the worst news of my life. Not only had I not gotten into a group with my Todd, but Mint had. And she'd also gotten into a group with Ava's crush. The whole thing felt rigged. I felt a note land next to my arm. It was from Mint!

These are such great groups!

What a terrible note to write to me. I drew a big frowny face on it and slid the note to the side of my desk so she could read it. Then another note landed next to my arm. It was from Ava.

You better make her dump that group.

But I didn't know how to make Mint do that. She was very independent and difficult. She'd already managed to steal two of my drawers when she didn't even have enough stuff to fill them. I didn't bother listening to who ended up in the final two groups. What did it matter to me?

"You'll work in your groups after lunch today when you'll receive your assigned novel section. But before that, I think it's time for a pop quiz."

My stomach felt nervous. We rarely had those. And I hated it when we did.

"Let's see what you remember about New Mexico's water resources."

That didn't seem like a fair thing to do on a Monday. Because, like most normal sixth graders, I was busy doing a bunch of stuff over the weekend that had nothing to do with remembering my state's water resources.

"I am so glad I reviewed this last night," Mint said as Mr. Guzman picked up a stack of quizzes from his desk.

"What a brownnoser," a voice said.

I flipped around to see who it was. Tuma! I nodded at him, but he didn't look at me.

I felt one more note land next to me. It was from Todd.

Maybe I'll get to come to your house to work with Mint.

I was almost happy to read that note. Except Todd should not have been coming over to my house to work with Mint. He should be coming over to my house to see me.

I couldn't wait for Angelina Mint Taravel to return to bear-infested Eagle River, Alaska, because that was exactly where she belonged.

· 13 ·

Lunch started out reasonably well that day, because as soon as we entered the cafeteria Mint told me that she wanted to take this time to get to know Kimmie a little bit better.

"Since we're going to be working together in this group, I think it makes sense to break bread with her," Mint said. She sounded as if she was forty.

"Wait! Did I read the menu wrong?" Rachel asked. "I thought they served vegetable flatbread sandwiches tomorrow. Did I miss it?"

For some unknown reason, that was Rachel's favorite lunch item at our school.

"Relax. 'Break bread' is a saying," Ava explained. "It means you share a meal."

"You know everything," Mint said, and there was a small ounce of sarcasm in her voice.

I saw a red color creep into Ava's cheeks. That was a mean thing to say, because Ava had just gotten a very low score on her pop quiz, whereas Mint had received a perfect one.

"I know the things that matter," Ava replied.

"Awesome," Mint chirped. "See you back in class."

"Later," I said, sounding a tad more insincere than I intended.

Mint flipped back around so fast that her hair lightly slapped her in the face. "I forgot. I hope the class captains like your cookies. They look so much better than your last batch."

"Thanks," I mumbled. It was a huge relief that she wanted to spend lunch with Kimmie.

Ava, Rachel, Lucia, and I all went and collected our bagels and returned to our regular table. I kept my cookies on the bench beside me, because I was worried that if I set them on the table that people seated near me would think that I had a bunch to share. Because I'd only made enough for the cookie basket.

"I'm so lucky that I passed that quiz," Lucia said. "Who knew my parents' love of visiting reservoirs would pay off one day?"

"That quiz was lame," Ava said. "Let's not talk about it."

There was a little bit of silence while we chewed our bagels.

"I'm really happy we're together," Rachel said to me.

"Yeah," I said. It was a relief to have one friend in my group.

"I'm actually a little bit worried about my group," Lucia said. "I don't want to get stuck doing all the work."

"Jasmine will help you," I said. "Both of her parents are doctors. She knows how to work hard on a team." I didn't mention her other team member's pork-chop scent.

Ava snorted. "I think it's pretty clear that I got the worst group of all."

There was no way to object to that observation. Because it was true.

"Paulette? Tuma? Bobby?" Ava shook her head. She was so upset I thought I could see tears welling up in her eyes.

"Bobby is smart," Rachel said. "He plays chess."

Ava rolled her eyes. "How is that going to help me write a wolf play?"

Then the table shook a little. Because Jagger and Todd arrived and put their trays down next to us with a lot of enthusiasm. It was a shocking and fantastic development. They never ate lunch with us. They always sat at the boy tables.

"Yo, guess who got a perfect score on the pop quiz?" Jagger asked. He stuck a fish stick in his mouth and bit it in half.

Nobody answered. We didn't want to say Mint's name.

"I did!" Jagger said.

That was news. He never scored well on quizzes or tests or art projects.

"And I have your cousin to thank for that," Jagger said.

"Did she let you cheat off her?" Rachel asked.

"No," Jagger said with a frown. "She sent me quiz texts last night."

Ava's eyes grew very big. I thought Mint had hijacked Jagger at my pajama party. But that was nothing compared to sending him quiz texts on a Sunday night.

"That's interesting," Lucia said.

"I did so bad," Todd said. "I wish Mint would have sent me some quiz texts."

I felt my heart beat very fast inside my chest, like a fluttery bird had gotten trapped where my heart used to be.

"Let's talk about something else," Ava said.

I took a bite of bagel and tried to think of another topic. *Crunch. Crunch.*

"So where's Mint?" Jagger asked.

Oh no. This was a horrible development. Jagger shouldn't ask for Mint in front of Ava. That was cruel. Lucia tried to save things.

"What do you think of the group assignment?" she asked.

Todd shrugged. "I hope we get a good part."

Ava pounced. She did not want anybody asking about Mint again. "What part would you want?"

Todd looked at the ceiling as if he was thinking really hard. "Remember the part where the girl was starving and so she ate raw meat *after* one of wolves chewed it for her and threw it up back up? Maybe something like that."

Gross.

"I forgot all about that," Jagger said.

Me too. My mind tries to forget gross stuff as soon as possible.

"Lane!" a voice called. It was a guy. My friends and I all started looking around.

"Derek is calling for you," Jagger said.

I felt my cheeks turn red. "It's about the cookies I brought."

"You brought cookies today?" Rachel asked excitedly.

"For the basket," I explained. "My vegan cookies."

Everybody looked a lot less excited once I'd said that. I was relieved when Derek stopped calling for me. He had bad timing. I was busy talking to Todd and Jagger.

"Let's talk about something besides our groups," Ava said. "Because I got the worst one."

We all looked at Ava in a pitying way. Except for Todd. Because he didn't know about the Ava/Jagger crush. So he missed out on the deeper meaning of what was being said with our eyes.

"But Bobby is smart," Jagger said. "He reads comic books from the seventies."

"And he plays chess," Rachel repeated.

"That doesn't make me feel any better," Ava said. "What about Tuma? And Paulette?"

Ava didn't call them losers in front of Jagger, but that was exactly what she thought of them.

"It'll be okay," Lucia said.

"I want to switch groups," Ava said. Then she looked up at Jagger and blinked several times.

It's as if I could read Ava's mind. She wanted Jagger to drop Mint from his group and invite Ava. But that couldn't happen for two reasons. First, Jagger didn't have the authority to do that. Second, Jagger obviously wanted Mint in his group. Ava kept blinking and blinking. The only reason she stopped was because Mint showed up to our table. With Kimmie.

"Jagger and Todd," Mint gushed. "Kimmie has some of the best ideas ever."

Ava's mouth dropped open.

"About our play?" Jagger asked.

"I don't think my ideas are *that* great," Kimmie said. She chewed on her lip a little and adjusted her glasses so they weren't slipping down her nose.

"Don't sell yourself short, Kimmie," Mint said. "Your strategy for building a wolf den that's fully functioning and yet still viewable for the audience is amazing. I mean, ah-maze-zing."

"Cool," Todd said.

It hurt my fluttery bird heart to hear that Todd thought her idea was cool.

"She sketched a diagram of it right here on this napkin," Mint said, thrusting a white rectangle inked with elaborate markings in front of Jagger.

"But you don't even know which scene you're getting," Ava said. "You might not even get a wolf den scene."

Kimmie looked down at the cafeteria floor as if she was super bummed to realize this.

"They might get a wolf den scene," Lucia said. "The main character spends a ton of the story in the wolf den."

Ava rolled her eyes.

"We've sketched some other stuff on napkins too," Mint said. "Possible ways to create the tundra using common household items: sheets, pillows, shower curtains."

What? I hoped Kimmie planned to let her group use her family's household items. Because I sure wasn't going to let Mint take our shower curtain.

"Let's go check it out," Jagger said. He picked up his tray and stood next to Mint. "And I've got some questions about the slime caves and the magic rock."

"But you haven't even been given your novel section yet," Ava tried again.

Mint let out a big sigh and looked up at the ceiling. "This suspense is brutal. I wonder if I went and asked Mr. Guzman for our parts if he'd give them to me right now."

"I highly doubt that," Ava said. "Highly."

"He said we'd get them after lunch," Rachel said.

"It doesn't hurt to ask," Mint said.

Ava snorted a little bit while she drank her milk.

"Hmm," Mint said. "We should totally take a few minutes right now and brainstorm."

"I bet whatever we get we'll need some tundra," Kimmie said.

"Okay," Jagger said.

"So how long have you been playing *Dwarf Massacre?*" Todd asked. "Jagger says you've conquered every level."

"Yeah," Mint said. "That game is awesome."

Ava looked down at her last bite of bagel and scowled while they all left in an excited clump.

"Your cousin is rotten," Ava said. "She just stole Jagger and Todd on purpose. Nobody is that excited about a transformational genre assignment."

"I can't believe she plays *Dwarf Massacre*," Lucia said.

"That is pretty unbelievable," I said.

"Did she get really good grades in Alaska? Is she worried about keeping up her GPA?" Lucia asked.

I shrugged. I did not want to have to lie about this. "Probably."

"Do you think that Mint likes Jagger?" Rachel asked. "I mean, as more than friends?"

Ava's eyes narrowed.

"He must," Lucia said. "I mean, he's texting her about New Mexico's water resources."

"Yeah," Rachel said.

Ava looked so miserable. It made me feel miserable too. Since my cousin was the source of her pain, I felt as if it was my job to say something to cheer her up. So I did my best to try to head off the drama.

"I'm sure it's nothing," I said. But even though I wanted to believe those words, deep down I had no idea whether or not they were true.

"What makes you say that?" Ava asked.

I glanced around the table at all the staring faces. And then I just started saying random things.

"I don't think she's interested in Jagger," I said. "She's just social."

Ava looked a tiny bit happier.

"She is very social," Rachel said. "She basically talks to anything with a face."

"True," Lucia said. "But she talks to Jagger a lot. Plus, they text."

Ava looked devastated again.

"Good point," Rachel said.

I watched Ava stare at her empty milk carton. She didn't deserve to have her feelings hurt. So I just kept saying random things.

"I think Mint has a crush on somebody back in Alaska," I blurted out, even though I had no idea. We'd barely talked about her life there.

"Really?" Ava asked. "Why do you think that?"

Hmm. That was a good question.

"Does she talk about him?" Rachel asked.

I really didn't want to lie. So I thought of a way to avoid doing that. "She writes in her diary every night like a fiend. And she's very secretive about it. She's probably writing about the guy she likes."

Lucia finished her bagel and then licked a crumb from her bottom lip. "Most people are secretive when they write in their diaries. It's where people put their most private thoughts. She might not be writing about a guy."

"Well," I said. "I think his name is Diego."

What was I doing? Why had the name of her cabdriver popped into my head? And why did I say it? It didn't matter. Ava looked almost happy. "You never told me that Mint kept a diary."

We heard Jagger's laugh echo through the cafeteria. Followed by Todd's. It was a painful sound to hear.

"I wonder what Mint writes about in her diary. Do you think she writes about us?" Rachel asked.

"Probably," Ava said. "We're very interesting. We would make a great reality show."

Jagger's laugh bounced through the lunchroom again. And then Mint zoomed out of the cafeteria.

"And she's probably writing about Diego," I added.

Everybody nodded. Which felt good. And bad.

"Do you know what would be fun to do this weekend?" Ava asked.

"What?" Rachel asked. "Work on our wolf plays?"

"No," Ava said. "Have another sleepover."

"Ooh! Maybe Jagger and Todd will bring donuts again," Rachel said.

"So fun!" Lucia said. "Let's do it."

"Yeah!" Rachel said.

"I'll ask my mom," I said. But I wasn't sure she'd let me have another sleepover so close to my last one. When it came to slumber parties, my mom believed in pacing.

When Mint and her huge smile came racing into the cafeteria holding a piece of paper, she looked like a happiness bomb had gone off inside her.

"I have our assignments!" she said, panting like a crazy person.

I couldn't believe that Mr. Guzman had given them to Mint.

"They are so great!" Mint said.

Within seconds, Kimmie and Jagger and Todd were clumped around us.

"Okay. Okay. Okay," Mint said. "This is the best assignment of our lives."

"Do you have everybody's parts?" Ava asked with a bunch of skepticism in her voice.

"Oh yeah," Mint gushed. "This piece of paper lists E-V-E-R-Y S-I-N-G-L-E P-A-R-T.

"Lane," Mint cheered, pointing an annoyingly happy finger at me. "You, Rachel, Kevin, and Felipe have the opening scene where she meets all the wolves."

"Ooh," Rachel said. "We could have done much worse."

"Lucia!" Mint said, her voice breaking with enthusiasm. "You, Jasmine, Thad, and Lexy got a crazy awesome scene!"

"What is it?" Lucia asked. Her eyes looked bigger than I'd ever seen them.

"It's, like, a double scene," Mint explained. "It's the part where Julie is starving to death and hunts the owlet and then watches the wolves take down the caribou."

Lucia licked her bottom lip and mulled over the idea. "That's a decent section," she said.

"Decent? I loved that scene! It reeks of survival," Kimmie said. "What did we get?"

Mint dramatically cleared her throat. "We have the section where the plane shows up and shoots at Julie from the air, because, dressed in her furs, she looks like a bear."

This news hit Kimmie like a birthday present. She was so thrilled she couldn't speak.

"I'd forgotten about that part," Jagger said. "It sounds good."

"We'll probably need an oil drum or something that looks like an oil drum," Todd said. "The moment when she tried to protect herself by crawling underneath it had a ton of suspense."

I was sort of surprised that Todd had read the book close enough to remember that part. He must have really liked Julie's story. Did he read other books like that? Maybe he liked the gunfire part because he liked stories with life-or-death drama. Maybe I should have talked about this with him. Maybe discussing the novel and all its conflict would have been a good way to further our relationship.

"Did Wren get a good part?" Rachel asked.

Mint lit up. "Wren, Wyatt, Coral, and Isaac have the flashback."

"The flashback?" Lucia said. "I don't remember the flashback."

Mint rushed to explain. "The second section of the book where Julie goes back in time to the life she had before the wolves. Not the part with her dad so much, but the part with her in-laws, Naka and Nusan, and Julie's terrible husband, Daniel."

I had forgotten that Julie had a terrible husband named Daniel.

"It was rotten when Julie was forced to make parkas for all the tourists," Rachel said.

"It was rotten when Naka turned out to be an alcoholic," I added.

"That book had a ton of themes," Lucia added.

The bell banged through the cafeteria and I started to stand up.

"What about me?" Ava asked.

Her voice sounded a tiny bit worried. It sounded so unlike Ava. So we all looked at her.

"Are you ready for this?" Mint asked, throwing her hands up over her head.

"Yes," Ava said.

"You guys have the awesome part where she meets the Eskimo family," Mint said.

Ava blinked. I guess she didn't think it was an awesome part.

"That's the only section without any wolves in it," Ava said.

It was pretty obvious that in addition to not liking her group, she didn't like her assigned section.

Mint shrugged. "I think it's a good part. I mean, it's a pretty emotionally charged scene. And some of it takes place on frozen river ice."

Other than mentioning the frozen river ice, Mint didn't try to sell Ava too much on the Eskimo scene. Mint looked revved and ready to leave. She took a bouncy step forward with her transformational genre group in tow. It made me sad to watch Todd leave with her. What good was having a relationship with a boy if you never spent quality time with him at school?

"School is so stupid this year," Ava said.

"It'll be okay," Lucia said. "That's not a terrible section."

"I think it has a sled in it," Rachel offered.

"Bleh," Ava said as she dumped her tray.

Then we walked into the hallway and heard something
that almost made Ava crumple.

"That's an amazing idea!" Jagger said. "Mint Taravel,
you are *so* cool."

"*Too* cool," Todd added.

I didn't know if they were talking about their project
or the dwarf game or something else entirely. Then we
heard Kimmie's mousy voice chime in. "Too cool for *this*
school!"

Ava stopped walking. I pulled on her arm to make her
keep going but she wouldn't budge.

"She's awful," Ava said. "She's ruining everything."

But she was only going to be here for a little while longer. I wish I could tell my friends. They would feel so much
better knowing that.

"Why can't Jagger see how terrible she is?" Ava mumbled so softly only I could hear. "And weird."

"I guess their personalities just mesh," Lucia offered.

But Ava didn't want to hear about their personalities
meshing. "No," she said. "It's because he doesn't see who
she *really* is!"

"Maybe," I said.

"I know what I need to do!" Ava said, pointing to herself. "I need to show Jagger Evenson exactly who Angelina

Mint Taravel really is. And once he sees that, he'll want to puke."

This didn't sound good. I felt Ava's arm slip through mine.

"We've put up with her weird, hijacking behavior long enough," Ava said with so much force that a little bit of her spit landed on my face. "Now it's time to destroy her."

Lucia and Rachel both looked shocked. I just wiped it away with my sleeve.

"Um," I said, thinking this over. "Destroy?" Did Ava really have time to finish learning her cello part for *Sleeping Beauty* and destroy Mint? I glanced at her index finger and spotted her callus. It was huge.

"Exactly. We need to have a three-way call and iron out our plan. You. Me. Rachel. Lucia."

"Isn't that a four-way call?" Rachel asked.

"Whatever," Ava said. "Saturday afternoon, I'll come to Lane's house and we'll call Rachel and Lucia and strategize from there."

"I'll ask my mom," I said. But I wasn't completely sure she'd say yes to this plan.

Then, as I was walking away with my friends, I felt somebody touch me. I was happy to see that it was Leslie. Because of all the Mint drama, I'd forgotten to look for them during lunch.

"Do you have a minute?" she asked.

Lucia, Rachel, and Ava waved to me. "See you in class," Ava said.

They understood that they couldn't hear us talk about important class captain stuff.

"I've got my cookies right here," I said, handing them the Tupperware container. "Sorry I didn't get them to you before school started." I wanted them to know that I was totally on top of things. Even though I'd failed to deliver my cookies to them this morning.

"These are vegan?" Robin asked, peeling back the plastic lid to sneak a peek.

"They are," I said.

"Nice job," Leslie said. "My mom made vegan cookies once and they looked like dog crap."

I was so happy I'd gone with the lemon-poppy-seed recipe.

"Now we have something else we need to talk to you about," Leslie said in a very serious voice. "Your cousin."

Robin raised her eyebrows and fixed her eyes on me in an intense way.

Great. Had Mint done something to upset the eighth graders? Robin took a break from staring at me in an intense way and glossed her lips.

"What's her story?" Robin asked.

I didn't know what they were after. "She's from Alaska," I explained.

"What happened to her parents?" Robin rubbed her lips together, smearing the gloss to distribute an even shine.

"What do you mean?" I asked. Did they want me

to talk about Aunt Betina's divorce? Her deadbeat ex-husband? Her new husband, Clark? That seemed invasive.

"Why did she move here without any parents?" Leslie asked. "That's weird."

I nodded. I had to tell them something. But I really hated lying to their faces. "Her mom just got remarried. They couldn't all move here at the same time. So they sent Mint first."

That seemed to satisfy them. And it was a minor lie.

"We like her," Leslie said.

"Oh," I said. That surprised me. Had they ever talked? When? Why would Mint be talking to the class captains behind my back and not tell me about it?

"She's so retro!" Robin said. "And I love how she trashes her clothes."

I wanted to inform them that she had actually trashed some of my clothes, and it wasn't cool.

"Well, that's it. See you at class-captain meeting," Leslie said. "Don't be late."

"I know," I said. There was no way I was going to be late to my first official class-captain meeting. I was counting down the days. As I walked to Mr. Guzman's class, Derek fell into step with me.

"She must be driving you nuts," he said.

I didn't say anything. Knowing that Leslie and Robin liked her, I didn't want to complain about Mint to another class captain.

"If you need to vent, you should call me. All last summer we had two of my cousins visiting from Peru. It was a nightmare," Derek said. "Complete life disruption." Then he made a sound like a bomb was going off.

We reached Mr. Guzman's door and I stopped. Derek's hair still looked incredibly plastic-y.

"Thanks," I said.

"Class captains need to stick together," he said, tapping me on the shoulder.

"Okay," I said. I really wanted him to leave so that Todd wouldn't see me talking to him and get the wrong idea. And Derek really needed to stop touching me. I didn't touch him.

"By the way," Derek said. "Your cookies look great."

"Um, thanks," I said, looking over my shoulder toward my classroom.

"They deliver the cookie basket to Ms. Knapp today. Hopefully, she doesn't back out," Derek said.

"Back out of what?" I asked.

"Being our faculty mentor. Apparently, last year's crew and their luau were too high maintenance or something," Derek said, leaning toward me a little bit.

I took a small step back. "Huh," I said. I wondered what would be the fate of the class captains if we lost our faculty mentor. "That sounds bad."

"Oh, it would suck. If we lose our faculty mentor, the school won't give us a budget to plan the parties. We'd basically lose our status."

"It would be totally rude of her to drop us," I said. I really didn't want to lose my status.

"I'll do whatever I can to make sure that doesn't happen," Derek said.

Standing in the hallway, I thought I could hear Todd's voice. "Bye," I said, trying to encourage Derek to leave.

"I'm out," Derek said as he flashed me a peace sign, and made his way down the hall.

· 14 ·

Having my best friend set out to destroy my cousin put a bunch of pressure on my home life. Because it made me feel conflicted. I didn't necessarily want Mint to be destroyed, I just wanted her to go back to Alaska and stay there and never have contact with me or anybody I knew, ever again.

On Saturday, I sat across the table from Mint, waiting for Ava to arrive. It was pretty awful. Mint kept going on and on about what a great time she was having at Rio Chama Middle School. But listening to her ramble about my school was only part of what was so awful about the meal. I also had to watch her put food in her undersized mouth. The meal felt like torture.

"I love the chili verde sauce!" Mint said as she inhaled another bite of breakfast burrito.

"Me too. That's why I make a whole bowl of it," my mom said. "I'll put it in our pork tacos tonight."

"Yum," Mint said as she smacked her lips in an annoying way.

Buzz. Buzz. Buzz.

"Phones aren't allowed at the table," I told Mint in a very judge-y way.

"Isn't that your phone?" Mint asked.

Did she always have to be right?

As I pulled my phone from my pocket, I saw Todd's name flash across my screen. I loved it when I saw his name!

"Who's that?" Mint asked.

She was so snoopy. And tricky. I suspected that Mint knew it was Todd and wanted me to admit that I had a relationship with him right in front of my parents. But I wasn't about to do that.

"Can you hand me another napkin?" I asked, ignoring her question.

Then I answered Todd's call. But I was already thinking of ways to speak to him without using his actual name.

ME: Hello there.

"Here's your napkin," Mint said.

My dad looked at me as if he expected me to take it. So I did, but when I took it, Mint tried to give it to my hand that was holding the phone, and I ended up dropping my phone. And it fell. And bounced. Into the chili verde!

"Augh!" I yelled.

Mint swooped in like a bird of prey and pulled my phone out of the sauce.

"I think it will be okay," Mint said, shaking the bigger pieces of green chili off it.

"Can you hear me?" I said into my phone. "Does my phone still work? Are you there?"

But when I pressed it to my ear, I couldn't hear Todd's voice, I just got a bunch of chili verde on my face.

"Power it off!" my dad yelled. He snatched my phone from me and turned it off. "You can't turn it on for a day. You need to make sure the circuit board is dry or you'll fry it."

"I think you caught it in time," my mom said. "And it didn't get totally submerged. Good job, Mint."

Good job, Mint? This whole thing was her fault. I felt so doomed. Not only had I hung up on Todd, but I couldn't call him back. Or anybody else. For at least a day.

"You can use my phone to call Ava back," Mint said. "Was it Ava?"

Man, I couldn't believe how obnoxious she was. "Let's not talk about this right now."

"Let's not overreact," my mom said. "It was just a phone. It will be fine."

"Mint was saying you were assigned a wolf exercise in school," my dad said.

"I believe it's called a transformational genre exercise," my mom said. "This would be the perfect opportunity for Mint to wear her wolf T-shirt."

Mint shot me an accusatory glance. But I shot her one right back. Then Mint took things one step further.

"I can't wear that shirt," Mint said. "I don't have it anymore."

"What?" my mom asked in a very concerned voice. "Did you leave it somewhere?"

I could not believe Mint was trying to get me into trouble. I thought back to the moment where I'd plunked that shirt in the trash can. It had felt so right. But now, with both of my parents staring at me, it felt so wrong.

"Where did you leave it?" my mom asked.

Did I really have to admit what I'd done? She ruined my shirt, so I threw hers away. We were even. Plus, her shirt was ugly.

"I left it at school and now it's just gone," Mint said, answering before me.

I didn't know how to feel about any of this. I mean, we shouldn't have even been talking about it.

"Well, we'll get you a brand-new one," my mom said.

"Absolutely," my dad added.

What a mistake!

"You are so thoughtful," Mint said sweetly. She was practically on the verge of tearing up.

"Forget about it," my dad said. "Tell me more about your assignment."

"Okay," Mint said. And then explained the assignment in a way that made it sound way cooler than it actually was.

Apparently, when it came to my school life, I could

never be the first person to tell my parents anything any-more.

"Sounds neat," my dad said.

It was hard not to stare at my phone on the counter. I missed it already.

"I find it incredibly well-timed that your class has been assigned a novel so appropriate for Mint," my mom said.

Mint nodded. "It is so much fun being the expert."

I rolled my eyes.

"Too bad Ava doesn't like her part," Mint said.

"Oh, Ava doesn't like her part?" my mom asked.

I did not want to gossip about Ava with my parents. "Can't we talk about something else?"

There was a little bit of silence while we ate and tried to think of something else to talk about. Then the doorbell rang and I was relieved, because it meant that Ava was early. I jumped out of my chair.

"I'll get it!" I said.

I noticed that Mint got up too. Which was weird. She didn't need to help me answer the door. It was my house. My life. My doorknob. I jerked open the front door and nearly died. It wasn't Ava. It was Todd. Why was he ring-ing my doorbell? Maybe that was why he'd called me. To tell me he was stopping by. A flood of happiness tumbled through me.

"Hi," Todd said, waving at me. "Is Mint here?"

"My study partner!" Mint exclaimed. "You're early!"

"Huh?" I asked. And all that happiness disappeared. Todd's coat brushed my arm as he entered my house.

Then my mom appeared and she was smiling, which I didn't like at all. Because she didn't even understand what was happening. One of the people I cared most about in the whole world had just entered my foyer and she didn't even know his value to me.

"My mom let me bring an old shower curtain for our tundra," Todd said.

Our tundra? They were seriously going to replicate Alaskan tundra together. Then I saw a familiar head appear out of the corner of my eye. It was Jagger.

"Jagger?" I asked. "You came to work on the project too?" They still had weeks before they performed it. I mean, Mint wasn't even going to be here. Didn't she feel bad about that? Knowing that she was going to abandon her group?

"Mint wanted to practice with her group," my mom said. "Didn't she tell you? I was under the impression that was why Ava was coming over too."

Something smelled fishy. Why would Mint invite my friends to my house and not tell me? Why wouldn't Todd tell me? I shook my head very slowly from one side to the other, trying to figure things out. "Ava isn't even in Mint's group. She's in a group with Paulette, Tuma, and Bobby."

"Oh," my mom said.

"You are going to nail that opening scene," Todd said. "So Mint, Jagger told me that you have a codebook to help us get out of the slime caves."

"It's not really a codebook," Mint said, twirling her hair

in a flirty way. "Just a notebook I kept of secret passage-ways and hidden potions."

"We've only found, like, three potions," Jagger said.

"And one of them melted our armor and turned us purple," Todd said.

"Oh," Mint said. "You found a bag of poison."

"Is this a video game?" my mom asked.

"Yeah," Jagger said. "It was basically my life all summer but now I'm stuck in a cave."

The doorbell chimed again. It was Kimmie. "I brought instructions and ingredients to make papier-mâché ice blocks."

Mint really, really should have told me this was happening.

"If you go with the no-bake papier-mâché paste recipe, we need to add salt to help prevent mold," Kimmie said.

"Awesome!" Mint said, giving her a high five. "We've got plenty of salt!"

"And I brought *Dwarf Massacre*," Jagger said. "If we want to take a break and play it."

"Totally," Mint said.

Then I watched Todd and Jagger and Kimmie and Mint all tromp into my kitchen. My house felt so invaded. Under normal circumstances, it would have felt awesome to have Todd in my kitchen. But under these circumstances, it did not feel awesome.

I kept standing by the door. Waiting for my life to feel normal.

"Is something wrong?"

I turned. Ava was standing on my front steps. Before I could answer her, laughter tumbled out of my kitchen.

"Who is that?" she asked.

Then Kimmie's voice boomed out of the kitchen. "You are so funny, Jagger!"

Ava's mouth dropped open. "Is Jagger in your kitchen?"

It wasn't as if I could hide what was happening. So I just leveled with her. "Yes. With Kimmie, Todd, and Mint. They just got here."

Ava looked like somebody had punched her in the gut.

"Why are they in your kitchen?" she asked.

"Good question. They claim they're making ice blocks out of a no-bake paste," I explained. "But I think their visit is *Dwarf Massacre Three*–related."

She lowered her voice. "Why didn't you tell me Jagger would be here? I would have worn a different outfit."

"I didn't know," I said. "Mint didn't even tell me."

"This is one more reason to destroy her," Ava said, her mouth settling into a hard line. "Let's go to your room."

"Don't you want to go in the kitchen and say anything to Jagger?" I asked. "Like, hello?"

Ava's eyes got big. "No way. I didn't wear lip gloss and my shirt has a giraffe on it. I didn't know I was supposed to look cute."

So we raced past the kitchen and straight to my room.

"This is unbelievable," Ava said.

"It's not ideal," I agreed.

Laughter floated down the hallway and into my room.

"Everything she's doing is calculated," Ava said.

"Maybe," I said. "Or maybe she's just trying to make a bunch of friends."

"Ugh," Ava said. "You don't really believe that and neither do I. Let's make our call."

Ava whipped out her cell phone and dialed Rachel and Lucia. Then she put her phone on speaker.

AVA: Let's not waste time. Okay. Everybody should know that Todd, Jagger, and Kimmie are in Lane's kitchen with Mint. And that Mint set this up behind Lane's back.

LUCIA: Wow.

AVA: It's like she doesn't understand how middle school even works. When you live in society, you still have to follow certain laws. Just because you might not have heard that killing a person is wrong doesn't give you the right to go out and murder anybody you want.

RACHEL: Wow. Murder is a powerful word.

ME: It really is.

AVA: If Mint and Jagger start going out, I'll die.

LUCIA: But she probably doesn't like Jagger. Lane said that Mint liked somebody back in Alaska. Diego?

RACHEL: Have you seen a picture of Diego?

ME: Um. No.

RACHEL: I wonder if Diego looks like Jagger.

(A bunch of silence while we thought about whether or not fake Diego might have looked like Jagger.)

RACHEL: Do you think Jagger likes Mint? I mean, *likes* likes Mint?

AVA: No! (series of gagging sounds)

LUCIA: Even if Jagger does like Mint and even if Mint does like Jagger, he lives in Santa Fe and she lives in Alaska.

ME: Along with Diego.

(I didn't know what was wrong with me or why I kept bringing up fake Diego. But the more I did it the easier it got.)

RACHEL: Sometimes long-distance relationships work. My aunt is dating a train conductor who lives in Wyoming. They're online constantly.

AVA: Don't tell me that!

RACHEL: Don't yell at me.

LUCIA: Yeah. Don't yell at Rachel.

AVA: Stop telling me what to do!

ME: Let's try to be more quiet.

Knock. Knock. Knock.

"We need to get some things," Mint said as she entered my bedroom.

"Look. It's Mint Chocolate Chip," Ava said in a voice filled with disgust.

"Am I interrupting something?" Mint asked, glancing at our faces.

"Yes," I said. "A phone call."

"We'll be quick," Mint said.

And then something happened that I never thought would happen in a million years. Kimmie entered my bedroom. Followed by Jagger. And Todd Romero.

"What do you need exactly?" Ava asked.

She tried to smooth her hair and smile a lot, because she looked most cute with flat hair and a happy face.

"We need a notebook," Jagger explained.

"And a pair of socks," added Kimmie.

"Why do you need socks?" Rachel yelled through Ava's phone.

"Because we're making seal fur mitts!" Kimmie yelled in the direction of Ava's phone.

"Hi, Mint!" Lucia's voice said. "This is Lucia."

"Hey, Lucia, what's going on?" Mint said coolly.

Ava shot me a hostile look. Which bugged me a little bit. Because I wasn't in charge of who Lucia said hey to when she was on speakerphone. Kimmie, Jagger, and Todd stood beside Mint as she pawed through her duffel bag.

"Is that your notebook?" Jagger asked, pointing to Mint's diary on the floor next to my bed.

"No, my notebook with my game shortcuts is yellow and has a sticker of a mortally wounded dwarf on it," Mint said. "That's my journal."

Ava glanced at Mint's journal on the floor and smiled at me.

"Maybe I put the notebook in my drawer," Mint said. "Can you look and see?"

"Me?" I asked. Mint shouldn't think she could boss me around in front of my friends.

"Todd," Mint clarified. "Could you look in my top drawer for me? And could you grab a pair of socks for Kimmie?"

"You're using your own socks, right?" Ava asked. "Because I'm pretty sure that turning them into seal fur mitts will ruin them. And you've already destroyed enough of Lane's clothes." She shot me another angry look. I know she wanted me to do more to confront my cousin, but I just didn't feel comfortable doing that in front of Todd. As much as I was on board to destroy my cousin's life, I guess I was hoping we could do it in a polite way.

"Of course they're mine," Mint said.

"Oops," Todd said.

Oops? I looked over at Todd. No way! I couldn't believe it. He hadn't opened Mint's drawer. He'd opened my drawer, and it was the one that had my underwear in it. Jagger glanced over and looked very uncomfortable. Todd was holding a pair of my polka-dot panties. What was he doing? I mean, there was no way you could confuse them with socks. I felt like I could die. Until Mint showed up, I never had to worry about a guy I liked suddenly dropping by and popping into my room and grabbing my panties by mistake. It was humiliating. I mean, that pair was super old.

"Those aren't socks," Kimmie said. "You should shut that."

Todd, now bright red, dropped my underwear and slammed the drawer shut.

"Sorry," Todd stammered.

"Oh, I think I told you the wrong drawer. Sorry, Lane!"

I was going to die.

"I found the notebook in my duffel bag after all," Mint said. "Back to practice."

My face felt so red and hot I almost couldn't breathe. As soon as they all filed out, instead of giving me a reassuring hug, Ava jabbed a finger at me.

"What just happened?" Lucia asked.

"Todd just dug through Lane's underwear drawer," Ava said.

"Shhh," I said. Hearing this news spoken out loud during our three-way call made it feel more embarrassing and terrible.

"Wow," Rachel said. "That's weird."

And hearing those words made me feel like crying. Because it was weird. And it never would have happened without the existence of Angelina Mint Taravel.

"Was it a cute pair?" Lucia asked. "Or did it say something crazy on them?"

"We are not having this conversation," I said.

"Why did you even give them permission to open your drawers?" Ava asked. "They were your property."

"Mint made me feel like I had to give her a couple of

my drawers," I explained. "She asked me in front of my parents and I had to say okay."

"You should never feel that way about your underwear drawer," Rachel said.

"Stop. Stop," I said. I needed to process what was happening. I felt very stunned and unhappy.

"I can't believe this," Ava said. "Mint is controlling your brain. Just like she's controlling Jagger's."

"I feel like I missed a lot of what just took place," Rachel said.

"That doesn't matter now," Ava said. "We need to rethink our strategy, because we're handling her all wrong."

I hoped Ava didn't want to do anything too violent.

"She's very savvy," Ava said.

None of us said anything for a whole minute. I think we were debating in our heads whether or not Mint was savvy.

"There is only one way to solve this!" Ava said.

"Stop screaming into the phone," Rachel said. "I need to turn down my phone volume."

"We need to let her seek her ultimate geek level," Ava said.

"Isn't she already there?" I asked. She had just left my room wearing socks on her hands, and ten minutes earlier, she'd helped Kimmie make no-bake paste.

"You're right. We need to set her up just like she set Lane up," Ava said. "We're playing way too nice."

"That sounds mean," Rachel said.

"Exactly," Ava said.

"I'm not sure about this," Lucia said.

But Lucia's waffling didn't slow Ava down. "We need to take her to a public place. And humiliate her."

"More public than school?" I asked.

"Yes!" Ava tapped her head while she thought.

"I know," Ava said. "The mall!" Then she released a crazy laugh that made my skin goose pimple.

"Really?" Lucia asked. "I hate the mall."

"And when I'm through with her, so will Mint," Ava said.

· 15 ·

Ava said that plotting the perfect revenge could take a few days, which seemed reasonable. Plus, her teacher was insisting that she hold her cello bow with a looser thumb and she was having a tough time with that. Unfortunately, her callus had gotten so big that if you were looking really closely, you could see it from across the room. But it wasn't a crisis, because Mint was still going to be around for a bit. Sigh.

I tried to pay as little attention to Mint as possible and to focus on homework and my friends and my class-captain duties. In fact, attending my first official class-captain meeting put me in a perfectly good mood. It was as if Mint didn't exist. Until the meeting started . . .

"Where is Ms. Knapp?" I asked. There were two big

pizzas on the table, but our faculty mentor wasn't around. Had she dropped us?

"She doesn't have time to attend the meeting," Leslie said, grabbing a big cheesy slice of pizza.

"But she's agreed to sign off on all our paperwork," Robin said. "So we're set."

"I am so excited to start planning our disco year!" Fiona, the fifth grader, said. "I even watched *Saturday Night Fever* with my mom."

Even though Fiona's comment seemed a little annoying, it also made me feel a tiny bit self-conscious. Because I hadn't been researching disco at all.

"Before we start, I have a question for Lane," Leslie said, aiming the point of her pizza slice at me. "And it's serious."

Oh, great. I felt totally unprepared to answer anything serious.

"What's going on with Jagger and your cousin?" Leslie asked.

Robin nodded like she wanted to know the inside scoop as well.

"He's my next-door neighbor and I've seen her over there six times," Leslie said.

It surprised me that Leslie was keeping track. But I figured I'd try to answer as honestly as possible. "They're working on a group project."

"Really? For school? Because kids from Red Rock Middle School are hanging out with them," Leslie said.

It was like Mint had this whole other life she was living outside of my house that I didn't even know about.

"That's news to me," I said, and bit into my slice.

"Maybe you could find out what's going on," Fiona said.

I wasn't about to take orders from a fifth grader. "Why?" I asked, trying to sound neutral.

Robin glanced at Leslie. They both looked upset. "I have a cousin that goes to Red Rock Middle School and they've heard about our disco theme. Did you tell them?" Robin asked.

"No!" I said. I couldn't believe I was being accused of being a squealer at the first official class-captain meeting.

"Well," Leslie continued, "your cousin told my cousin that you told her."

My mouth dropped open. I was stunned. This level of dishonesty and betrayal was totally intolerable cousin behavior. "I never said a word," I insisted. "I swear."

"It's not like I want to accuse you of lying or anything," Robin said. Though that was basically what she was doing.

"Well, that's good. Because I'm not lying," I said. "I have no idea how the Red Rock kids know."

"She sounds really sincere," Fiona said.

"That's because I'm telling the truth," I said. "You should not judge upperclassmen." I pointed right at Fiona. I couldn't believe a fifth grader was talking to me like that.

"I really want to believe you," Leslie said.

"Me too," Robin said.

"But why would your cousin lie?" Leslie asked. "You know, I used to like her. But now I think I was wrong."

I really felt like I needed to throw Mint under the bus.

"You know," Derek said. "Jagger lives near me too. I'll drop by and get to the bottom of it."

He was so kind.

"That would be great," Robin said. "Because if they're going to start blabbing about our disco theme to everybody, we need to change it now."

"Got it," Derek said. "I'll check it out this weekend."

Robin smiled. "Let's move on to something awesome. Leslie and I have made a major decision about our disco theme."

I was so excited that we were finally getting to the party planning. That was ninety percent of the reason I wanted to be a class captain.

"Part of what sucked about the luau was that people wore togas and weird non-luau costumes," Leslie said with a frown.

"Yeah," Robin said. "People dressed against theme. And I don't think it was totally deliberate. I think our student body needed more guidance."

They made a good point. In addition to the toga costumes, I remembered at least three sixth graders who came to the luau dressed as grapes.

"So this year we're going to give them that guidance," Leslie said.

Fiona squealed with excitement. "Are we going to travel

from class to class and offer disco demonstrations while wearing funky costumes from the seventies?"

Wow. That did not seem like a fun thing to do. I looked up and caught Derek staring at me. I think he agreed with me, because he was shaking his head.

"Better!" Leslie chirped. "We're going to tell people to come to the party dressed up as moods."

"This makes loads of sense," Robin explained, "because during the seventies people were obsessed with mood rings."

"Totally. People were really plugged in to their emotions," Leslie added.

I had never heard of mood rings before. Maybe my mom knew what they were.

"So Robin is going to be fierce. And I am going to be fun." Leslie jerked one of her thumbs at Robin and the other one at herself.

"Will we assign moods to every student?" Fiona asked. "Do that many moods exist?"

Leslie shook her head. "Great question. We're going to have a master mood list. And people can design their costumes using that."

"There's so many moods," Robin gushed. "Trippy, theatrical, urgent, groggy, rebellious. I could go on for an hour."

"But she won't," Leslie said. "Okay. So we have assigned moods for the class captains, because that seemed important." She turned to Derek. "You're going to be dreamy."

Derek cocked his head in confusion. "What costume works for that?"

"You don't have to do much," Leslie said. And then she blushed.

"And, Fiona," Robin said. "You're going to be sweet."

Fiona beamed at this announcement. "I love that!"

"And, Lane," Robin said. "We were totally divided between two moods for you. So we're going to let you choose which one you want."

Leslie interrupted. "You're a complex person. It's a total compliment that we couldn't decide."

"Okay," I said. I'd never thought of myself as having one defining mood, let alone two.

"We were torn between cerebral and organic," Robin said.

I blinked. How did either of those moods fit me? "Really?" I asked. Maybe they were just joking.

"We thought cerebral because you're smart and deep," Leslie explained. "And organic because you have an earthy style."

"Plus, your vegan cookies really spoke to an earthy mood," Robin said.

"But I was *assigned* vegan cookies," I said as a way of mild protest.

"Yeah. And you totally nailed it," Robin said.

Then the door creaked open and interrupted this rotten news. I was totally surprised to see Ava.

"Just getting my cello," she said. "I have to leave early for practice."

"Cool," Leslie said.

"Hey!" Ava said in a sharp way. "Did one of you guys move my bag? It's totally upside down!"

I glanced around to see people's reactions. Everybody looked confused.

"Is that a problem?" Fiona asked.

"If it's damaged it sure is," Ava snapped as she picked up her big canvas cello bag and tried to right it.

"Do you need any help?" Derek asked, standing up.

Robin shot him an angry glance.

"I don't want anybody touching my cello," Ava said. "I can't believe this."

"*We* can't believe this," Leslie responded. "We're having an important meeting."

Ava looked at our pizza and rolled her eyes. "I need to inspect it and see if it's been damaged."

Ava was really holding things up. Couldn't she do that in the hallway? I needed to object to my assigned moods before it looked like I'd agreed to one of them.

"How do you inspect a cello?" Robin asked.

Ava unzipped the bag and carefully removed the large wooden instrument. It was glossy, and the scroll at the top looked like a curling wave. I didn't think it looked damaged.

"Give me a second," Ava said, taking her bow out of its protective case. "I need to rosin the hairs of my bow and play it a little to make sure it's okay." Then she rubbed the bow against a cake of rosin.

"I'm pretty sure it's okay," Leslie said.

Ava frowned and touched the tuning pegs on her cello, then positioned the end pin on the floor and placed the instrument between her legs. "Let me play the beginning of Tchaikovsky's *Sleeping Beauty*. And then I'm out of here. By the way, it's a waltz."

I thought Ava was acting like a spoiled person. She did not need to play the cello in the middle of our class-captain meeting. But she did it anyway. She laid her bow across the strings and lightly pressed her curled hand against the fingerboard. She released one continuous deep sound. Then she repositioned the bow at a sharper angle and the sound changed. After a few times drawing her bow across the strings, she lowered it and plucked the strings with her thumb. "It's okay," she said.

Then she carefully repacked the cello in her carrying case and zipped it back up.

"This is really starting to bug me," Robin whispered to Leslie. "We're losing valuable time."

Over the years, I'd heard Ava play at roughly a dozen concerts. Usually, my mom came. My mom always said she thought the cello sounded like dark chocolate melting.

"I didn't mean to freak on you guys. But my cello is one of the most important things in my life," Ava said.

"It's cool," Derek said, answering for everybody.

"Yeah," Robin added. "It's fine. Bye."

"Have a good meeting, Lane," Ava said. Then she put her pinkie near her mouth and thumb near her ear and made the universal sign for "Call me."

I nodded.

"She's totally gifted," Fiona says. "I bet she gets a scholarship to college."

I'd never thought of that, because I didn't spend any time thinking about college. But Fiona was probably right. Ava was gifted. She was lucky. And after Mint moved back to Alaska, I hoped Jagger could recognize this.

"I wonder who moved her cello," I said.

"Maybe it was an accident," Fiona said.

"Or maybe somebody wanted to mess with her," Derek said.

I took another bite of pizza and considered that. Who would want to mess with Ava?

"What mood do you think Ava will dress up as?" Leslie asked.

That question caught me off guard. I didn't automatically think of my friends as moods. "Um, intense?" I offered.

"Ooh!" Robin gushed. "I like that! We should add it to the list."

"And what about you?" Leslie said. "Cerebral or organic?"

I wanted to say neither. As I mulled over how to respond, I could hear myself breathing. When I tried to imagine dressing up as a cerebral mood, all I could picture was a slimy brain. The last thing I wanted was to show up to our first big school party looking like a frontal lobe or cerebellum. Those costumes wouldn't be cute. "Organic," I heard myself say.

I figured it was the better of the two moods. With this much time to plan and prepare, I could use any free time I had searching online for the perfect costume. I wanted to wear something cute enough to catch Todd's attention and make him look at me and say "Wow!"

· 16 ·

The weekend after the class-captain meeting, I was looking forward to spending a day with my mom. The mother-daughter outing was her idea. To be honest, I think she felt guilty that she'd spent so much energy on Mint. But I figured that now that my cousin would be flying out of town in a week and a half, my mom was just trying to get things back to normal.

"I think I want two tacos," I said. Normally, when we went to Mijos Tacos I just got one. But I was in the mood to indulge.

Mint sat at the table doing homework. I know it was petty of me, but I felt thrilled that we were leaving her behind with my dad.

"Do you want us to bring you back a taco?" I asked. I

was impressed with myself for being such a thoughtful person, especially in light of the current circumstances.

Mint looked up from her social studies book and shook her head. "That's okay. I'll probably just eat at Todd's."

What? Why would she be eating at Todd's? Was she going there? Normally when she worked on her project she went to Jagger's house. Why would that suddenly change? I narrowed my eyes. Mint was so devious. I'd been eavesdropping on her phone conversations all week and I'd heard her tell Jagger that Kimmie was going to visit her grandparents in Tucson and so they were taking the weekend off from working on their project. So why go to Todd's?

"Why would you eat at Todd's?" I asked.

"Um," she said, looking up and me and tapping the eraser end of her pencil against the table. "Because we finally got him and Jagger out of the slime caves and they're ready to board the pirate ship and conquer the remaining Iron Dwarves."

I didn't understand any of that. "You're going to hang out at Todd's and play video games?"

Mint nodded. "Once I finish my homework."

And I just snapped. Even though I should have shown more maturity, I stomped my foot like a five-year-old. "That's not happening!"

My mother came into the kitchen carrying a basket filled with our clean laundry. "What's wrong?"

"I want to go to Todd's with Mint!" I screamed.

My mother looked very surprised. "Honey, we've got plans to get tacos together."

Mint was so underhanded. She'd orchestrated the whole thing. I really couldn't stand her.

"But I want to go to Todd's!" I said. If only I could have explained to my mother how much Todd meant to me.

"You need to stop yelling," my mom said. "Do you want to help me fold clothes and we can talk about this?"

I shook my head. "Not really." Because we folded clothes in the family room, so Mint would be able to hear everything we said. I wanted privacy. "I want to talk to you *alone*. Can we go to the garage?"

My mother looked surprised as she set down the laundry basket and joined me in the garage. I was surprised myself. Maybe this *was* the time to tell my mom that Todd and I were basically going out. What was the worst that could happen? I was practically a teenager now. Of course I was going to start having boyfriends. She had to understand that, right?

But then I thought back to something Ava once said concerning parents and guys and dating: "Don't ever tell you parents you're going out with Todd. You've got the kind of parents who would go into lockdown. Trust me. Keep it a secret as long as you can or your life will turn to suck."

Once we were in the cool darkness of the garage, I felt pretty vulnerable and unsure about whether I really wanted to have a heart-to-heart with my mom about Todd.

I figured I'd keep it simple. "I really want to go to Todd's too."

My mom sighed and put her arms around me. "I know. But I think it's important that Mint spread her wings a little and have some independence during her stay with us."

What was wrong with my mother? What made her think that? "Okay," I said. "But I don't understand why I can't go too."

My mother patted me very sympathetically. "You've got your friends and now Mint has hers."

I pulled away from her patting. I was so offended. They were my friends first! And my mom was really not seeing the bigger picture: there was no reason at all for Mint to be visiting my boyfriend's house without me. "Please?"

My mother shook her head. "I feel it's important to let Mint have this."

I felt differently. "Fine," I said, stomping back inside the house. As soon as I entered the kitchen, I was stunned by what I saw. Mint was looking at my phone. I felt totally violated. "Get away from my phone!"

"I was moving it away from the water pitcher so nothing would get spilled on it," Mint explained. She set my phone down on the counter and slowly backed away from it.

I shook my head. I didn't believe her.

"I don't even know your code!" Mint said.

But Mint had proven herself to be a savvy person. I bet she did know my code. "Sure you don't!"

"I don't!" Mint said.

"Girls, stop yelling," my mom said.

"This is unbelievable," I said. "I'm getting in trouble for getting mad at Mint for snooping through my phone?"

"I didn't," Mint said. "I promise."

Then I realized how the Red Rock kids had learned about the disco theme. Mint had read the texts Robin had sent me. And then she'd squealed about it. She. Was. Rotten.

"You read my texts and found out about our school's disco theme and you told the kids from Red Rock Middle School and now the other class captains think I squealed and have a blabbermouth cousin!" I had never been this mad before.

"That's not how it happened!" Mint yelled. "You told me about it once in the middle of the night. We had a big conversation. I promise. I never read your texts. Have you ever considered that you might be a sleep-talker?"

What? Was she being serious? I wasn't a sleep-talker. "Stop telling ridiculous lies!" I walked toward Mint because I wanted to take her phone away from her and read all her texts so she would see how it felt.

"I don't know how we got here, but I am breaking this up," my mom said, grabbing me by the wrist and leading me down the hall. "Lane, stay in your room. I'm taking Mint to Todd's house as planned. When I come back, we'll get tacos and talk through this."

My mother was siding with Mint! Unbelievable. "I don't want to get tacos anymore." I slammed my door. But I still stayed next to it so I could hear what my mom told Mint.

"You cannot touch Lane's phone ever again," my mother said.

"I didn't read her texts," Mint said.

"I believe you, but Lane worked very hard to be class captain and she takes it seriously."

"I know. She's a great class captain!" Mint gushed.

And what my rotten cousin said next, I'll never know, because the only sound I heard after that was the front door closing. She was gone. Off to Todd's. It took every ounce of self-control I had not to call him and tell him what a lying, dishonest, sneaky person Mint was. But I held back. I knew Ava was hatching a great plan. And I also knew that she was better at conniving than I was. So, hard as it was, I decided to take a deep breath and be patient. Because I didn't want to spoil what Mint had coming.

· 17 ·

The weekend was filled with silence, because I had little interest in talking to Mint or my parents. When I finally got back to school, there was only one person I wanted to see: Derek. I found him at his locker looking into a small, square magnetic mirror. He was fluffing his hair.

"Hi," I said.

When he turned around, he seemed pretty excited to see me.

"What's up, Lane?"

Derek lifted his hand in the air, expecting a high five. I wasn't the kind of person who went around high-fiving guys in the hallway, but I did it anyway.

"I'm here for an update about Jagger and my cousin," I said.

Derek shut his locker, looked over his shoulder, and then back at me. "It was really weird."

"It was?" I asked. That was not the report I'd been expecting. Because while I knew Mint was weird, I had no idea Jagger was too.

"I don't have time to cover everything before class," he said.

"Then we'll be late," I said. I reached into my pocket and pulled out a tardy slip. "We're class captains. We get certain privileges. Remember?" Three weeks ago, I never would have said such a thing to Derek or anybody else. But Mint was forcing me to reorder my priorities. I was also surprised by how serious my voice sounded.

"Okay," he said. "Let's not do this in the hallway. Let's go to the meeting room."

"We can do that?" I asked.

"Sure," Derek said. "Mrs. Archibald loves me. Most secretaries do. I'll just tell her it's an impromptu class-captain meeting."

Suddenly, I was on a power trip. Of course I could go with Derek to the meeting room and claim I was taking part in an impromptu class-captain meeting and gossip about my cousin instead of going to class. As soon as Derek flashed his smile, Mrs. Archibald let us have the meeting room. We shut the door and sat down, and Derek spilled all he'd learned.

"They're not doing what you think they're doing," Derek said.

I didn't know if I was prepared to hear the truth. "So they're not working on the wolves project?"

He shook his head.

"And they're not playing the dwarf game?" I asked.

He stopped shaking his head and looked up. "They do that a little, but they do something else a lot more."

Poor Ava. If Mint and Jagger were super serious, Ava would die. My stomach would not stop flipping. "Okay," I said. "Tell me."

"They're roller-skating," Derek said. "Like maniacs."

"Huh?" Why would they be doing that? I didn't even know Mint owned roller skates. What was going on?

"They're pretty serious about it," Derek said. "Other people join them. It looks like they have choreographed moves."

"Are you sure you're spying on the right people?" I asked. "You have witnessed Jagger Evenson group roller-skating with my cousin?"

"Yeah," Derek said. "And this last weekend, they were at your friend Todd's."

My heart started beating so much faster. "You saw them at Todd's?"

He nodded.

"And they were roller-skating there?" I asked.

He shook his head. "No, they were playing that dwarf game. I think they won. There was a lot of celebrating."

This was so much information to process, and I wasn't sure how much of it was useful.

"Is that everything?" I asked.

"No," Derek said. "I've got one more thing to tell you."

I wasn't sure I could handle one more thing. "What?"

After I asked that question, I noticed that Derek looked nervous. His eyes darted around the room and then finally settled on me. "Never mind."

What was wrong with Derek? Why wouldn't he just tell me?

Ring. Ring. Ring.

When the bell rang, I jumped a little.

"We should go," he said.

"But what else do you need to tell me?" I asked.

Derek got up and didn't answer me.

"Derek?" I said. "It's rude to say that you've got something to tell a person and then not do it."

He made his way to the door in silence and I followed behind him. What a perturbing turn of events. Guys were *so* frustrating. Derek opened the door to the hallway and looked back at me.

"You're a lot cuter than your cousin," he said. "That's what I wanted to tell you."

I froze. Even after Derek started to walk away, I just stood there. Did Derek *like* me? Did I want Derek to *like* me? I wasn't totally sure. But I didn't think so. This was nuts. *When did Derek start liking me? Should I say something? If I don't, will the next time I see him be super awkward?*

"Wait!" I said.

Derek turned back around. "What?" he asked. "Do you need me to get more inside information for you?"

This moment felt so bizarre. I didn't know how I'd

missed the signs that Derek had liked me, and I also didn't know how I'd turned a fellow class captain into my cousin-spy.

"Thanks," I said.

"For trailing your cousin?" he asked.

"For that and for what you just said. It was nice." I smiled at him. I figured that was what you did in situations like this.

"So do you want me to stop gathering information?" he asked.

Derek was so good at info gathering that it didn't make sense for him to stop.

"Just be careful," I said. "Don't let them know what you're doing."

"Don't worry," Derek said. "I was born careful."

And then the bell rang again and I raced down the hallway to Mr. Guzman's classroom and my desk, which sat kitty-corner from Todd's. Which was where I belonged.

· 18 ·

Basically, I stopped talking to Mint at school and so did Ava. Lucia and Rachel were still polite, which made me feel a little bit betrayed. But I couldn't control what they did. And I couldn't control what they thought of Mint. All I could control was what *I* thought of Mint. And I thought she sucked.

It took days, but Ava finally figured out a punishment. She wouldn't tell me the details. All I knew was that it was my job to get Mint to the mall without any adults around. It seemed like something I could manage. Ava assured me that Mint wouldn't be physically harmed but that she would learn a very important lesson about loyalty and honesty and kindness. And she wanted the police to be involved. When she first told me this over the phone, I was pretty hesitant.

I said, "No police."

She said, "Some police."

I said, "Absolutely no police."

"One police officer. Maybe not on duty."

I yelled, "Ava, involving the police is taking things too far!"

She yelled back, "We at least need mall security!"

I tried to calm down and consider this.

"Fine," I finally agreed.

"Cool," Ava said in a happy voice. "But keep in mind that I can't control whether mall security calls the police for backup."

I felt like such a sucker.

Before we had a chance to implement our mall attack, my parents made the tragic and foolish decision that Mint and I should end our feud. And in a show of complete cluelessness about how this should happen, they took us to play miniature golf at a super family fun center. My parents didn't understand how sixth graders operated at all.

"My ball is never going to make it through that windmill," I said. The blades kept knocking my golf ball at the exact wrong moment, sending it into a pile of woodchips.

"Aim for the blade," my dad said.

That seemed like a terrible strategy.

"I can't believe you go back to Alaska in less than a week," my mom said to Mint.

But I could totally believe that. I was thrilled.

"We'll all miss you so much," my dad said.

This was so lame I inadvertently made a gagging sound. Luckily, that was the putt that sent my ball through the windmill.

"I'll miss you a lot too," Mint said. "My life back in Alaska is going to be so different."

That idea made me happy. Because my life was going to be so different too. It was going to be Mint-less. And I couldn't wait.

"I'm not even going to live in the same house," Mint said.

"Really?" my mother asked. "I didn't realize you were moving in with Clark."

"Yeah," Mint said. "At first, the plan was that he'd move in with us. But somewhere between Rome and Tuscany, they decided it made more sense to move in with him. My mom told me the other day."

"That's a big change," my dad said. "But maybe it will turn into a fun adventure."

That seemed like a cheesy thing to tell a twelve-year-old being forced to relocate to a new home.

Mint shrugged as if she didn't care much. "He lives a lot closer to town, which will be good because I'll be around stuff to do."

I watched as Mint's ball sailed between the windmill blades on her first try. Stupid family fun center. I scowled at the hole as Mint's ball approached.

My mother stood next to me and tapped my shoe with her club. "Stop being so dour," she whispered.

I knocked her club with my club and it made a loud clinking sound. "I don't even know what 'dour' means," I whispered back.

"Lane and I will meet you at the Abominable Snowman," my mom said.

That was the next hole, so I took my ball and followed her to the tee.

"This is one of the last family times we'll have with your cousin," my mother said.

"I know," I said, and gave her a huge grin. Didn't she understand that I hated every second of being with her?

"You're being mean, Lane Cisco," my mother said. "I realize that she disrupted your life a little bit, but you should still be nice to her."

Disrupted my life a little bit? She ruined it! And Ava's! Because she stole Jagger. But I had a feeling that if I told my mom this, she wouldn't even care. Instead of siding with Ava and me, she'd probably side with Mint.

"I'm being as nice as I can," I said, shrugging.

My mother dropped her yellow ball on the tee and set it in place with her shoe. "In a lot of ways, your cousin was given an unfair shake. I'm surprised you can't be more sympathetic."

I thought about Ava and our plan to destroy Mint. Maybe getting mall security involved was a tiny bit too severe.

"I've shared all my friends and introduced her to a ton of people," I said. Which was basically true. Except my best friend and I had both decided to hate her openly.

My dad came walking up with Mint. "So we have to get our shot through the Himalayas and the Snowman's legs?" he asked, sounding way too enthusiastic.

"Can I skip this hole?" Mint asked.

That was so unfair. Just because you encountered a tough hole didn't mean you could skip it. "Sure," I said. "But you have to take the six-stroke maximum."

"That seems high," my mom said.

But right next to us was a sign with the rules painted on it, so I pointed to that. "It's rule number two."

Mint nodded. "I'll take the six-stroke maximum."

This made me feel slightly better, because it meant her score wouldn't totally clobber mine.

"Are you getting tired?" my mom asked. "We can get a snack."

It was so frustrating to watch my parents cater to Mint's every need.

"I'm not tired. I just really do not like Abominable Snowmen."

What a lame excuse. This was the toughest hole we'd encountered.

"Why not?" my dad asked. "Is he seen as a dangerous character in Alaska?"

Mint shook her head. "Not really. But when I was a kid, I used to have the worst nightmares about the Abominable Snowman. I'd be walking along a snowy mountain path, and I'd see him. He'd be tall and furry like an ape and I'd just know he was the Abominable Snowman."

"He'd be walking? How was this a nightmare?" I asked.

If Mint was going to suck all the attention, she at least needed to tell an interesting story.

"He was so big and he'd walk in this really exaggerated way," Mint said. I watched as Mint tried to imitate the walk of the Abominable Snowman. She looked exceptionally weird and other people started watching our golf group.

"Sounds pretty scary," my mom said.

I shrugged. "I've had worse."

"What made it a nightmare was that the way he walked would trigger an avalanche. And the snow would just be drowning me. I'd try to swim to stay on top, but eventually I'd be covered. The whole world would be dark. And I'd be all alone."

"That is a terrible nightmare," my dad said. "A guy in my grounds crew lost a brother in an avalanche. Snowmobiling without a radio transmitter in Utah. Terrible way to go."

Mint nodded as if she was truly terrified. "And then, sometimes, I would hear voices above me. People I knew. Like my mom. And they'd be calling for me, their footsteps would crunch the snow above me, but I'd be trapped too far down. So I couldn't scream back. Pretty soon the voices would fade and I'd still be stuck there, running out of oxygen."

"I think that's the worst nightmare I've ever heard," my mother said, wrapping a supportive arm around Mint.

Which hurt my feelings a little bit, because she once told me that I'd had the worst nightmare she'd ever heard when I told her about my dream of accidentally fastening myself to my birthday kite and sailing into the sky and hitting electrical wires. So which was it? Whose was worse? Mine or Mint's? I was on the verge of asking when my dad said something shocking.

"In honor of that nightmare, I think we all scratch this hole and take the six-swing penalty."

"Absolutely," my mom said.

Even at a stupid miniature golf course, Mint managed to get everything she wanted.

"But I want to play this hole," I said. I pointed to the rounding tops of the Himalayas and the terrifyingly hairy legs of the Snowman.

My dad reached over and took the ball out of my hand. "Show some solidarity."

"We're not missing anything. The hole after this one is a sand castle with three drawbridges and several sand dragons," my mom said.

"Yay," Mint cheered.

Awroo! Awroo! Awroo!

A simulated wolf howl erupted from my phone. I dug it out of my pocket as quickly as I could. As a joke, Ava and I had personalized some of my ringtones. I'd forgotten all about giving Todd the sound of a gray wolf.

"Is that your phone?" my dad asked. "It sounds like an injured dog."

"It's a wolf howl," Mint said.

"It means it's an important call," I said.

"Hello?"

But Todd wasn't there.

"Can you get reception in here?" my dad asked. "I'm roaming."

I needed to escape this place and call Todd back. I had a life to live, and couldn't waste all night in a family fun center with Mint. She wasn't fun. And I didn't really consider her my family.

"Hey, Mom and Dad," I asked, sounding as polite as possible. "Do you mind if I step outside and return that phone call?"

Neither my mom nor my dad looked fine about this.

"We've got six holes left," my dad said. "Winner gets an ice cream sundae."

"That's okay," I said. In my mind, I was trying to figure out what Todd wanted to talk about. I'd already figured out what I wanted to talk about with him.

"We need to finish what we started," my mom said. "We came as a family and we'll play as a family. To the end."

The way she said this and pointed at me made me realize that I couldn't easily excuse myself to go and talk to Todd. It was so unfair.

Awroo! Awroo! Awroo!

I couldn't believe Todd was calling me again. "At least let me go outside and send a text," I said.

But then my mom snatched my phone away from me. "It's your turn to putt over the drawbridge."

"Mom," I said. "You made me accidentally hang up on my friend."

Then my mom looked at my phone. And she saw that

the call was from Todd. She seemed a little surprised. I think she'd assumed it was from Ava or Lucia or Rachel.

"You can text your friend Todd when we're finished," my mom said. "And that's final."

I watched as she slid my phone into her pocket.

In the history of owning my phone this had never happened to me before. Mint had turned my life to suck. And I didn't owe that girl anything.

· 19 ·

What happened next was almost too weird for words. That night, after finishing the miniature golf game and getting trampled by Mint and texting Todd without hearing anything back, I went to sleep and had the worst nightmare of my life.

I was walking along a snowy mountain path on my way to visit Todd. And on the path coming the other way was the Abominable Snowman. He was big and hairy and sort of yellowed with age. He walked exactly how Mint had described, and it didn't take long before his big footsteps triggered an avalanche. I swam through the snow, trying to stay on top of the big chunks of ice, but it didn't work. I wound up pinned in total darkness, surrounded by walls of snow.

I was terrified. I tried to scream, but my mouth kept filling with snow. And then I heard footsteps. Was it my mom? My dad? Ava? No! It was Todd. I heard him calling for me.

"Lane? Lane?" he yelled. "Where are you? Why won't you text me back?"

As hard as I tried, I couldn't scream. The words wouldn't come out. Then I heard a second voice. It was Mint! I knew nightmares could be terrifying, but I hadn't realized they could also cause nausea.

"I can't find Lane," Todd said. "Have you seen her?"

"I'm down here," I tried to yell. But my cries couldn't be heard.

"No," Mint said. "Want to come over and play *Dwarf Massacre Four*?"

"You own *Dwarf Massacre Four*?" Todd asked, sounding thrilled beyond belief. "It hasn't been released yet."

"I got my hands on an early copy," Mint said. "*The Reign of Pain*. It just arrived today."

"Cool!" Todd said.

Crunch. Crunch. Crunch.

I heard their footsteps fade into nothingness. And my heart broke.

When I finally woke up, gasping for air, I was incredibly relieved to see that it was morning and that Mint was already up and gone. Where? I didn't know and I didn't care. I raced to look at my phone to see if Todd had texted me back. He hadn't. This was so crazy. A relationship between two normal people who liked each other shouldn't be this hard. And that was when it hit me: even though it was a Saturday, Todd and I needed to talk right now. There was no reason to hide what we had. It was time to be official.

I threw on some cute clothes and ran out to the garage. I hadn't ridden my bike in weeks. I pushed against the tires with my thumb to check their air pressure. They felt great. I didn't question what I was doing. I didn't even ask my parents for permission. I strapped on my bike helmet and was off.

I didn't start getting really nervous until after I rang the Romeros' doorbell. When Todd opened the door, I was so ready to talk to him that my entire body felt electric.

"Lane," he said. He looked as surprised as I felt. "Did you get my text?"

I shook my head. My reaction confused him.

"Why are you here?" he asked.

That was a good question. I thought as fast as I could for the best possible answer. "I thought we could hang out."

He didn't appear freaked out by this answer. I thought that was a good sign.

"Want to watch TV?" he asked.

It was incredibly exciting to walk into Todd Romero's house. We entered his kitchen and he introduced me to his mom. Her wavy hair looked exactly like Todd's, except longer. And she was so tall and pretty. She was standing at the counter sorting a big pile of mail. I liked how both of her wrists were lined with thick, colorful bracelets. She was such a stylish mom.

"This is Lane," Todd said. "Mint's cousin."

That was a terrible way to introduce me. But I didn't say anything.

"Mint's cousin?" Mrs. Romero said. "I bet it's nonstop fun living with her."

Where had she gotten that crazy idea? I nodded. It felt so wrong that Todd's mom associated Mint with fun. But it felt even more wrong that she could associate me with Mint. How long would it take people to forget her once she was gone? A week? A month? A year? I hoped it wasn't a whole year.

"We're going to watch TV," he said.

"In the living room?" his mom asked.

"Yeah," he said.

As we walked to the living room, it did bum me out a little bit that Todd didn't walk right next to me. He walked ahead of me, like he was in a hurry. I felt confused. Did he want to walk ahead of me? Or did he think I wanted him to walk ahead of me? Or did he not even notice that he was walking ahead of me? Were his feelings about me changing? We'd only talked about our status one time. Before school started this year, he'd said, "It feels like we're going out." I'd said, "Let's not be official yet." He'd said, "That's cool." But did he still think that was cool? It seemed like now would be a good time to talk about whether or not we should take the next step and become official.

I sat down on the floor next to Todd, and he flipped on a show about alien hunters in Delaware.

"Do you ever watch this?" he asked.

I wished I could have said yes, but I had no idea that

people hunted aliens in Delaware. I watched his hand as he adjusted the volume on the remote control. Watching this, I was struck by a powerful feeling: This was Todd's life. These were all the things he touched throughout the day. This is where he lived and slept. This is the living room where he called me on the phone. This is the television I sometimes heard in the background.

"You'll love this show," he said, crashing down beside me. "These hunters are nuts."

It was really hard for me to focus on the show at all. I couldn't stop looking around. Family pictures hung on the walls. Were those old people riding the Jet Ski his grandparents? There was a stack of magazines by the couch. Shelves lined two walls and were crammed with books.

"Do you need something?" Todd asked me.

I didn't know how to answer that. Because I did need something. I needed him to talk to me. So I reached out and touched him. And when I did, this electric zap of static traveled through me and onto him. We both got shocked. Hard.

"Ouch," he said as he kept watching the show.

I decided to just ignore that fact that I'd zapped him. "Can we talk?"

"Sure," Todd said. "Do you want me to turn off the TV?"

One of the alien hunters released a blood-curdling scream.

"Maybe," I said.

Todd clicked off the power. But before we could talk, his phone rang. "It's Mint."

Uh-oh. I didn't want him to tell her I was here.

"Don't tell her I'm here," I blurted out.

He nodded. And they only talked for a few seconds before he hung up.

"What was that about?" I asked, even though saying that question made me feel nosy.

"She said the papier-mâché ice blocks don't need a third coat of paint. That they look awesome."

I was so sick of this stupid group work. "You know, the assignment is only worth a hundred points. That's only four vocabulary tests. Don't you think your group is going a little overboard?"

Todd shrugged. "Mint and Kimmie do most of the work. It's sort of fun."

"Fun?" I asked. It was as if the whole world had started defining that word differently than I did.

"Yeah. We hang out. Play my dwarf game. I store the props. No big deal," Todd said.

"Um, right," I said. Even though I thought it was quite a big deal.

"I'm lucky you have such a cool cousin," he added.

And that was when I decided that not only did I need to have a talk with Todd about our status, I also needed to let him know that Mint was not who he thought she was. But I didn't want to do this in the middle of his living room, where anybody could walk in and hear me complaining. So I made a suggestion.

"Maybe we could talk in your room," I said. But then I realized that sounded weird. "Or your backyard." But then I worried that that sounded just as weird.

"I don't think we can talk in my room," Todd said.

And then it was pretty clear that he was starting to feel uncomfortable, so I dropped it. "I know. I wasn't being serious," I said.

"Okay. What's up?" Todd asked me, looking around like he was already ready for me to leave.

But when he asked me those words, I didn't know quite where to start. I wanted things to go back to the way they were. And I also wanted us to be official. But I didn't know how to ask for any of that.

"Would you ever teach me how to play *Dwarf Massacre*?" I asked.

Did I really want that?

Todd smiled. "Sure. You're interested in playing? You're so lucky. Mint is an expert. She knows the game inside and out. The video game company chose her to test the next game for bugs before it's released. *Dwarf Massacre Four: The Reign of Pain*."

A chill went down my spine.

"Did you say *Reign of Pain*?" I asked.

Todd nodded. I couldn't believe it. It was as if my nightmare was coming true.

"Are you going to play it with her?" I asked.

"Totally," Todd says. "We've already synced it up online so that when she goes back to Alaska we can keep playing."

What? I'd assumed that once Mint went back to Alaska,

she'd be gone. I didn't think she was syncing with people. I kept hoping that once she left, people would forget about her. But if they became super connected online, then she might stay in contact with them forever. The horror!

"Do you want to play right now?" Todd asked.

Buzz. Buzz. Buzz.

I looked at my phone. The text was from Ava.

Ava: We're set. Can you get Mint to the mall today? Or tomorrow?

I looked up at Todd.

"I have to go. Can I take a rain check?"

"Totally," Todd said. "I love teaching people how to destroy steel dwarves."

"Cool."

And I loved that we were about to destroy Mint.

· 20 ·

Getting Mint to agree to the mall was incredibly easy, because for some unknown reason, she was very excited to go. She even chose a specific time for Sunday. Three o'clock. And before we went, she took a stupendous amount of time braiding Ava's ribbon pajama belt into her hair. Which I didn't even try to discourage. If Mint wanted belt-hair, I would stand aside and let her have it.

It was weird. Before Mint arrived, I would've thought belt-hair made you look ridiculous. But somehow Mint made it look almost okay. Even Kimmie and Paulette had started braiding thin pieces of fabric into their hair.

"Isn't this the cutest shirt ever?" Mint asked me as she spun around in the living room.

Mint was wearing a blue shirt that she'd painted with

big fluffy yellow birds. I don't even know where she'd gotten this shirt. I wouldn't have put it past her if she'd just found it on the street. It was that ugly.

"I wanted to add red birds too," Mint said. "But I ran out of puffy paint."

Who puts red birds on their clothes? How much puffy paint does Mint buy in a year? Isn't that stuff bad for the environment?

I didn't understand my cousin. Why did she want to make her clothes look weird? In the end, I decided these were useless questions. I needed to keep my hands off Mint. And let her seek her geek level. Which I suspected was hardcore dweeb.

When my mom dropped us off at the mall, she gave us the same rules she always gave me when she dropped me off with my friends.

Rule 1: Stay in a group.
Rule 2: Don't talk to anybody you don't already know.
Rule 3: Keep your phone turned on.
Rule 4: Don't buy anything that costs more than ten dollars.
Rule 5: Meet her at the same place where she dropped us off at the prearranged time.

But before she drove off, she called me over to her window and added one thing.

"If you see anything that would make a good bon

voyage gift for Mint, text me a picture and we'll consider it," she said. "We need to get her something meaningful. Something cool."

"Yeah," I said. Which wasn't really the truth, because there was no way I was going to look for a present for Mint.

"And also consider who we should invite to her going-away party."

I didn't even respond. I went into a deep hole of denial and pretended my mother had not uttered those words.

Mint skipped into the mall like a very happy person. It annoyed me. Before she got here, I used to really enjoy meeting my friends at stores. We'd have the best adventures ever. And we usually bought cool earrings and stared through the glass at the tattoo store and evaluated intricate designs of koi fish and dragons and skulls and weird-looking lions we would never get. But now we didn't have time to do that because we had to destroy Mint. So instead of having a fun mall adventure, we had to get to work.

"Let's go to the Belt Barn," I said. Because that was where we were meeting up with everybody.

"Let's swing by the Diamond Zone first," Mint said.

Why did Mint need to look at the Diamond Zone? That was where people bought wedding and engagement rings.

"Ava is probably waiting for us at the Belt Barn," I said. In addition to destroying Mint, Ava was crazy excited to find a new ribbon belt. She wanted a pink one to replace the one Mint had taken. Ava wouldn't even consider taking it back because she thought it was contaminated with Mint's head oil.

"Can we text her?" Mint asked.

Hmm. I didn't know what to do. I didn't want Mint to get suspicious, so it seemed like I should give into her a little bit.

"Okay," I said. So I texted Ava.

Me: Mint wants to meet at the Diamond Zone.

Then I noticed that Mint was texting somebody. But she tried to hide the phone from me. I really hated this. Because it made me worry that she was texting Todd or Jagger. "Who are you texting?" I asked.

She smiled at me. "How about I tell you after we finish shopping?"

What? That was ridiculous. She should just tell me now. I had a right to know.

"I'd rather know right now," I said.

But she didn't have time to answer me. As soon as we arrived at the Diamond Zone, we ran into Jagger. She had been texting him! And she'd arranged to meet him at the mall. It was almost like they were going out. Wait. Were they going out? When Ava saw this, she really was going to die.

"Hi, Mint," Jagger said. "Thanks for meeting me here."

And then I saw the craziest thing ever. Jagger hugged Mint and her cheek touched his cheek and I think I saw Jagger turn his head and give her a quick kiss. WHO DOES THAT? Even Todd and I didn't kiss each other on the cheek. We just wrote notes and held hands every couple of weeks. Cheek kissing at the mall in front of the Diamond Zone? My life felt like a soap opera. No. Mint's life felt like a soap opera!

"Lane!" Ava said as she rushed to my side.

By the panic in her eyes, I could tell that she'd seen the cheek kiss. Plus, it was probably going to be more difficult to destroy Mint with Jagger around.

"I need to go to the bathroom," Ava said. "Will you come with me?"

I really didn't enjoy going inside the mall bathrooms. They stank. But I agreed to do it anyway. For Ava.

"Are you going to wait for us?" I asked Mint.

"How about we meet you at Saddle Express," Mint said.

"Why?" I asked. "They sell saddles."

"And you don't own a horse," Ava said in a harsh way.

"I need to buy some saddle oil for my dad's birthday," Jagger said.

"And Saddle Express has a great selection," Mint said.

So Mint knew about Mr. Evenson's birthday? Interesting.

Ava grabbed my hand and squeezed it so tight that I could tell the exact words going through her mind. *I am dying. Mint is acting like his girlfriend.* I needed to get Ava out of here before she had a total meltdown.

"Okay," I said. "We'll meet you at Saddle Express. Bye!"

I practically tugged Ava's arm out of its socket as I dragged her down a side corridor.

"I am dying," she said as we approached the bathrooms.

"Wait," I said. "Do you want to sit by this planter?"

"No," Ava said. "It's surrounded by people. I don't want *people* to know about my problems."

"But the mall bathrooms stink," I said. Then I pinched my nose to emphasize this. "And as long as we don't talk too loudly, it'll be fine."

Ava didn't object because she was beyond upset.

So we sat at the planter and Ava started pouring out her heart.

"I have liked Jagger since second grade," she said. "He is such an awesome person. Big heart. Cute hair. Sparkly eyes. And he runs faster than anyone in soccer *and* baseball."

Jagger did run very fast and had sparkly eyes.

"And he wears the cutest shirts. And the most awesome shoes. And I love the way his voice sounds when he laughs."

"Yeah," I said. I hoped it made Ava feel better to empty out her feelings.

"No," Ava said, sniffling. "You don't understand. Jagger has two laughs and I love them both. He has a laugh that's sort of fake. Like when Todd tells a joke that really isn't that funny but Jagger laughs anyway."

I thought Todd's jokes were always funny. But I didn't say anything.

"And I love his real laugh. It's soft and easy, like he's swallowing a smile," Ava said tearfully.

Ava tried to imitate it, but she started to cry so hard that she mostly just released a croaking sound. She sounded so sad. Her feelings for Jagger were much more serious than I realized.

"What am I going to do?" Ava asked.

"I don't know what to say," I said. "Mint goes back to Alaska this week."

"But don't you watch movies?" Ava asked. "This is like a terrible love story. Where two people meet at a very young age. And then get separated by a million miles. But they stay in touch. And then years later they find each other on the Internet. Or maybe they wind up in the same high school. And bam! They reunite and become a couple again."

I'd watched a lot of movies. But I hadn't seen that one. Before I could think of something helpful to say, Rachel came over.

"Why are you crying?" Rachel asked.

Ava's cheeks were wet. "Because I came to the mall to destroy Mint, and instead she destroyed me."

"How were you going to do that?" Rachel asked.

The plan to destroy Mint had been a little mean, so it was almost a relief that it didn't happen.

"I was going to slip a bracelet in Mint's pocket and then alert mall security. She would have gotten in serious trouble. That plan made sense. I sort of felt as if Mint deserved to be in serious trouble."

"Wow," Rachel said.

"I know," Ava said, releasing more sobs.

"Don't cry," Rachel said. "Give me your hand. Do you want me to draw a squid on it?"

"That won't make me feel any better," Ava said. "It will make you feel better because you like drawing squids."

"Yeah," Rachel said. "Do you want to go watch a funny movie? Do you want a snack? What do you want?"

Ava shook her head and sniffled. "I want to un-see what I saw."

"What's going on?" Lucia asked.

We were all so worried about Ava.

"Mint and Jagger just met in front of the Diamond Zone and basically kissed," Ava said. "And then they went to buy Jagger's dad a birthday present."

Lucia gasped.

"Mint is way too young to be kissing guys at the mall," Lucia said.

"And what about Diego?" Rachel asked.

I really wished Rachel would stop bringing up fake Diego.

"They hugged and their cheeks touched, but I don't think they kissed," I said.

"Wow. Sounds like they're going out," Lucia said.

"Well," I said. "There's not really anything we can do about it."

"Sure there is," Ava said. "We can stalk them through the mall."

I was pretty sure Rachel and Lucia would resist this idea.

"Okay," Rachel said. "Can we get some ice cream first?"

"Hopefully they go into the Earring Shack," Lucia says. "It's BOGO today."

Then, as if we didn't understand what BOGO meant, because sometimes Lucia did use a vocabulary that was bigger than the rest of ours, she spelled it out for us. "It's buy one, get one free."

"Let's go," Ava said. "We need to catch them at the saddle store and follow them from there. If they're really going out, I need to witness everything with my own eyes."

This did not seem like the best idea Ava had ever had, but we all agreed to do it.

"They're totally just friends," Rachel said, forming her lips to the top of her ice cream cone and taking a bite.

"Why are they spending so much time looking at vitamins?" Ava asked.

We stood on the other side of the mall's courtyard and surveyed Mint and Jagger as they slowly wandered the bottle-packed aisles of the Nutrition Nook.

"Most people should take a multivitamin," Lucia said.

Lucia was way too sensible.

"They're leaving!" I said, crouching down a little.

"Let's hide in this store," Ava said, tugging on my arm.

Before I knew it, Ava tugged me inside a store that I'd never shopped in before. Bra Universe.

"We need to get out of here," I said.

My mind flashed back to Todd opening up the underwear drawer. The last thing I needed was to be found in a bra store. I didn't want people from my school to think I was obsessed with bras and panties. Because I wasn't. I barely thought about that stuff. It embarrassed me.

"These are actually cute," Lucia said, pointing to a

mannequin sporting a bright pink bra and panty set emblazoned with crystals.

"Stop pointing at that mannequin's butt," I whispered. I knew in my heart that going to the mall shouldn't feel like this.

"They've been there for twenty minutes and they're not buying anything," Ava said.

"Maybe they haven't found what they're looking for," Lucia said.

"No," Ava said. "It's like they're just wasting time."

Rachel took another huge bite off the top of her ice cream and slurped out a response. "Maybe they're just hanging out."

Ava scowled at Rachel. "Can you suck that thing more quietly? I don't want to get thrown out."

"Sure," Rachel said, delicately pecking at the cone with her mouth.

Ava squished up her face in what appeared to be a mixture of confusion and disgust. It's like I could read her mind. *Why would a guy want to hang out this long with Mint?*

"Duck!" Lucia said. "They're coming this way."

I knew it. They were going to spot me in a bra store.

"Wait," Lucia said. "They're stopping."

We all moved closer to the glass front wall of the store.

"They're sitting down," Lucia said. "Look! They're taking off their shoes."

"Gross," Rachel said. "I'd never walk around the mall in just my socks. I bet all the floor grime would turn them black."

"They're putting on different shoes," I said. From their backpacks, Jagger and Mint each pulled out another set of shoes.

"Those aren't shoes," Lucia said. "They're roller skates."

"You can't wear those in here!" Ava said. "It's against mall policy."

"Maybe Alaskan malls don't have those kinds of mall policies," Rachel said.

"Maybe Alaska doesn't even have malls," I said.

"Even so," Ava said. "Jagger should know better." She stared on, looking concerned, and exhaled some huffy breaths. "They're going to look like huge nerds if they try to roller-skate through the mall. I mean, don't you think they'll get caught by mall security?"

"Probably," Rachel said, nibbling very quietly on the edge of her waffle cone.

"They might be able to escape mall security if they can skate fast enough to a door," Lucia said.

"They're pretty far away from a door," I said.

"We should stop him," Ava said.

When we decided to let Mint seek out her geek level and then destroy her, we'd never imagined that she'd drag Jagger down to dweeb status with her.

Ava started to bite her nails, which she never did. "He's on the verge of becoming a complete loser! In public!"

I could tell Ava was reaching her breaking point, but I was still pretty surprised when she lunged toward the store's entrance. Luckily, Lucia held her back.

"I don't think you should do that," Lucia said.

But it was worse than any of us realized. Ava looked completely out of her mind. Her eyes were huge and panicked and very focused on Jagger. Ava had lost it. Gone bonkers. Nuts. Insane. Unzipped. I guess I knew this was possible: Mint's relationship with Jagger had driven Ava crazy.

"He could get accused of disturbing the peace. Or disorderly conduct. Aren't those misdemeanors?" Ava asked, looking at Lucia.

"I think so," Lucia said.

"That would go on his permanent record. My parents would never let me date somebody who'd committed crimes."

If they committed a crime, odds were that Mint and Jagger would get busted. The mall crackdown had started a few months ago after Tuma and Bobby attempted to skateboard from store to store. One day, the mall was just a fun place you could go and act goofy without any consequences. But following the skateboard incident, where Tuma collided with a Seeing Eye dog and the person it was guiding, the shopping center had posted signs listing strict rules that could result in fines, penalties, and jail time. Roller-skating and skateboarding were among them.

Rachel took another bite of ice cream. "Does Mint even know how to skate?"

I nodded. "She's been skating like a maniac for weeks."

"Really?" Lucia asked. "At your house?"

"With Jagger," I explained.

"How come you never told me about this?" Ava snapped.

And then it happened. Ava literally snapped. While I stayed ducked down behind the glass, Ava broke free from Lucia's grip and raced out of the store. The last words I heard her say were, "You suck! You suck! You suck!"

But Ava didn't get very far. She was barely out of Bra Universe when the loud music began to pound through the mall.

Do, do, do. Beep. Dun, dun, dun. Boop.

And then something really crazy happened. A big group of at least twenty people arrived on roller skates. They wheeled right up the mall's center court and formed a circle. And Jagger and Mint joined them. Then they started skating together. And lifting their arms up in unison.

"They're dancing," a woman standing next to us said.

Rachel and I wandered out of the store and stood next to Ava and Lucia. Soon everybody had wandered out of the stores.

"It's a flash mob!" Rachel said.

Except for a video I'd seen on the Internet, I had never seen a flash mob before.

"They're pretty good," Lucia said. "Look at the dude in the red skates. He's great at crossovers."

The dude in the red skates *was* pretty good at doing crossovers. He picked up his right leg and crossed it in front of his left. Over and over. Making the turns look super easy. And Mint and Jagger were pretty good too. They could skate forward and backward, and they seemed to know all the choreography.

"I feel like barfing," Ava said. "And I haven't even eaten in hours."

"Mint must have practiced a ton," Rachel said.

"Yeah," Lucia said. "Look at her shoot-the-duck!"

I couldn't believe what was happening in the mall's courtyard. Mint was unrecognizable to me as she leaned forward, lowered herself to a crouching position, balanced herself over one foot, and slid her other foot out in front. When had she decided to learn to do that? In Alaska? In New Mexico? And how had she hooked up with this flash mob?

Before Mint arrived, my life had far fewer questions.

"It makes me sick to watch this," Ava said. "I mean, these people are totally breaking the law and should get arrested."

"I don't think anyone's getting arrested," Lucia said. "It looks like mall security is keeping the skating zone clear."

And they were.

"I think this is a PR move," a man behind us said. "The mall has gotten so much bad press about reducing mall go-ers' personal freedoms that they wanted to stage an event where people could express themselves."

"Really?" Ava asked. "Where did you hear that?"

"My son is one of the skaters," the man said. "He told me about it."

"Who's your son?" Lucia asked.

"Jagger Evenson," the man said.

Ava's mouth dropped open and she just stood there.

"He's been practicing with his friend from Alaska," he offered.

I thought it was pretty good that Mr. Evenson had referred to Mint as Jagger's *friend* and not *girlfriend*. Lucia put her arm around Ava and gently redirected her stare to the skaters.

"We don't have to watch the whole thing," I said. It seemed wise to declare our spy operation over and just try to shop.

"She is so slick," Ava said as Mint switched direction in unison with Jagger and they both began skating backward.

"Does Diego roller-skate?" Rachel asked me.

"Probably," I said.

"Look! A news camera," Lucia said, pointing to a local camera crew set up on the other side of the mall. What a terrible thing to see. Three weeks in Santa Fe and my weird cousin had managed to make it on television. Maybe this had been her intent the whole time. Show up to my ordinary town acting like a super nerd by braiding a belt to her head and knowing five million things about Alaska. And then find a way to get on the local news with my best friend's crush. Maybe Mint was way more calculating than I realized. She certainly was a far better skater than I'd realized.

The flash-mob routine ended in a burst of energetic circle skating. All the mob people zoomed in a curve in front of me so fast that their mismatched outfits began to blur.

"We don't have to watch the whole thing," I repeated.

"Is that your mom?" Lucia asked me, pointing across the mall to a person near the camera crew.

It was!

She held her phone up and snapped several pictures. I couldn't believe my mom had known that Mint was going to be in a flash mob at the mall and hadn't told me. I couldn't even trust her anymore.

Ava turned around and looked me right in the eye.

"You should feel so betrayed," she said.

And she was right.

"Woot! Woot!" Mr. Evenson cheered as all the skaters came to a dramatic stop by lowering themselves to the mall's floor.

As people began to disperse, I tried to keep my vision on Mint. She looked so thrilled. So free.

"Is she holding Jagger's hand?" Ava asked, placing a hand over her mouth.

"Maybe they're just helping each other up," I said.

But they continued to keep their hands linked as they skated to a bench off to the side so they could change out of their skates.

"It totally looks like they're going out," Lucia said.

"Poor Diego," Rachel said in a sad voice.

"Poor Diego?" Ava said, her voice tense with pain. "Poor me!"

· 21 ·

Is it possible to live with somebody you no longer trust or like? Even for five days? I didn't think so. After the flash-mob incident, I avoided Mint as if she was made of poison. During the hours that followed the catastrophe at the mall, where Mint wrecked Ava's heart, every time my cousin entered a room, I left it. And at dinner that night, I ignored everything she said. And when I settled into bed that night, I scooted so far to the edge of the mattress that right before dawn, I fell right off my side of the bed and onto the floor.

"Are you okay?" Mint asked in a groggy and concerned voice.

Okay? OKAY? How could she not see that I basically hated her? In less than a month, she'd trashed my life. How could she be so selfish?

"Are you on the floor?" Mint asked.

Why couldn't Mint give me back my life and just shut up?

"Are you mad at me?" Mint asked as I slowly crawled back into bed.

I didn't say anything at first. I just slid between my sheets and listened to the silence.

"Lane?" Mint asked. "Are you hurt?"

I couldn't believe she kept talking to me. Wasn't it clear that I didn't want to have a conversation? Mint was so clueless!

"Can't you just shut up?" I asked, yawning.

And we didn't say anything else the rest of the night.

Avoiding Angelina Mint Taravel became my only goal. I arose before dawn and collected my things and got ready in the living room. While my mom and dad gushed at breakfast about Mint's roller-skating performance, I requested to eat my toast and eggs in the living room, underneath the light of our most powerful lamp, so I could finish my homework. On the bus, I read through my vocabulary list. *Adapt. Allegiance. Anguish. Awe.* Once we got to school, I ditched Mint and just sort of drifted all by myself.

Drift. Drift. Drift. Except, when I got to my locker, something happened that made it impossible for me to drift anymore. *Mint. Mint. Mint.* Everyone was talking about her. And Jagger too. Not only were they the topic of every conversation, images of them kept popping up on everybody's cell phones. I guess the footage had been featured on the nightly news. And circulated. And posted on the Internet. As the youngest skaters in the flash mob, she and Jagger were now basically celebrities. They'd gone viral!

"Have you seen this?" Lucia asked me, holding up her cell phone, showing me a website featuring the flash-mob footage.

"I'm sort of over it," I said.

"One hundred thousand people have looked at it on this site alone," Lucia said. "It's nuts."

I glanced at the picture of Mint zooming backward and then gracefully turning back around.

"And have you read the comments?" Rachel asked.

This made me jump a little, because I didn't even know that Rachel was there.

"So many people think Jagger and Mint make the cutest couple," Rachel said.

I glanced around to see if Ava was nearby. Luckily, she wasn't. Because she should not hear terrible things like that. It would only wreck her more.

Rachel dragged her thumb across Lucia's screen, scrolling through the comments. "They use a bunch of weird skater lingo."

I peered over her shoulder and read a few of them about Jagger and Mint.

The rexing couple is my favorite.
Those two out-scissor everybody.
They are both great at trucking!

Love it when they shoot the duck.

Too cool!!!!!!

The hardest thing about skating is the floor.

"Five more days and I am done with her," I said. "I don't care if she's great at rexing or not."

I wasn't sure I could make it through five more days.

"You can make it," Lucia said.

She was right. My mind turned that idea over again and again. One. Two. Three. Four. Five. I'd lived through five days before. A lot. Plus, I'd survived chicken pox. Stomach flu. Poison oak. Severe sunburn. I could survive Mint. I just needed to handle the rest of her stay the same way I handled all those terrible illnesses: one terrible day at a time.

Lucia and Rachel could tell how stressed out I was. So they each gave me a hug. I took a deep breath.

"Let's go in there and get this over with," I said, pointing to our classroom.

"It's probably going to be way better than you think it will be. Mint isn't evil. She's just really different," Rachel said.

That did not make me feel better. When was Rachel going to see how terrible my cousin really was?

When we entered the classroom, the first thing I noticed was how clueless Jagger seemed to be about all the drama unfolding around him. What was wrong with him? Couldn't he recognize drama? He sat at his desk reading a comic book, as if nothing had changed. *Everything had changed.* Not only did the whole world know he could roller-skate, but everybody at our school now thought he was going out with Mint. Was he? Shouldn't he clear this up? For Ava? For me? For Mint? For himself? For everyone? Was he just going to walk around all day and pretend he didn't have to address this issue? What a terrible thing to put Ava through.

And where *was* Ava? Lucia walked me to my seat and kept looking around. After I glanced at Ava's empty chair ten times, I saw Todd walk up to Mint.

"Pretty awesome trucking," Todd said. "And I love your orange wheels."

He loves her orange wheels. That seemed like a pretty disloyal thing for Todd to say to a person I pretty much hated and considered a traitor.

As my classmates settled into their seats, Mr. Guzman didn't waste a second of pre-class time. He hustled right up to Mint's desk.

"Wonderful skating," he said. "I'm incredibly impressed. I'm hoping you might talk a little bit about your experience after our quiz. Let's hope our link works."

"Sure," Mint said.

Gag. A link? Was he going to make us watch it?

Then he handed out a list of definitions, and we had to come up with the words and spell them correctly. But it was hard to focus, because while we worked on the assignment, Mr. Guzman lowered the projection screen, then brought a snarl of cords into our classroom and began untangling it.

I stared at my quiz. I stared at the cords. *Quiz. Cords.*

Cords. Quiz. Each definition seemed to get harder and harder.

3. devotion or loyalty to a person, group, or cause: *allegiance*
4. an emotion variously combining dread, veneration, and wonder that is inspired by authority, or by the sacred, or sublime: *awe*

Focus. Focus. Focus. Why couldn't Mr. Guzman stop fooling around with that cord? Why didn't he tell us exactly what we were going to watch? Usually he told us. My mind would not sit still. *Quiz. Cords.* And where was Ava? I looked back at her empty desk.

"Two more minutes," Mr. Guzman said. "And then we get to watch two of our class members demonstrating a very unique talent."

I shot a glance at Jagger. No way. You show up to one stinking flash mob at the mall and suddenly you're the coolest person to ever exist at Rio Chama Middle School. This had gotten out of control.

"One more minute," Mr. Guzman said.

I rushed to scribble the last of my answers. *Anxious. Arid. Agony.* Before I knew it, Mr. Guzman was standing alongside my desk, collecting my quiz. Luckily, I had finished. Luckily, I'd stared so hard at all the words on the bus that I thought I'd gotten a perfect score. And then, even though I had no desire to watch it, Mr. Guzman played us the footage of the roller skaters at the mall.

"I haven't seen rexing this impressive since I lived in Los Angeles," Mr. Guzman said, giving Jagger a thumbs-up sign as he moved to the back of the class to turn off the lights.

I closed my eyes so I didn't have to witness it again. Hearing the music was bad enough. But then I heard something way worse than the music.

"Isn't that Lane and Rachel?" Kimmie asked.

"Isn't that Lucia and Ava?" Paulette added.

I opened my eyes. Oh no! If you looked across the mall, on the other side of the skaters, outside Bra Universe, you could clearly see all four of us: me, Ava, Rachel, and Lucia. And if people were watching closely they could have spotted us actually inside the store. I couldn't decide whether we looked like bra shoppers or total stalkers. Or maybe we looked like bra stalkers! Any one of them was terrible. We were totally recognizable, standing in the store's front window, pointing and gawking at the flash mob, surrounded by a sea of bras. I wanted to die.

"What were you doing at Bra Universe?" Tommy asked.

Laughter rippled through the class.

"Let's watch your talented peers," Mr. Guzman said. "It's a rare moment, usually only glimpsed during ballets and rhythmic gymnastics performances, when this much coordination and dedication meet in one place."

"It is pretty amazing," Rachel said.

I shot a look at her. What was she doing? I shook my head. Things were beyond being out of control. I needed to do something. So I got out two pieces of paper. Because

I needed to write two notes immediately: one to Lucia and one to Todd.

Do you know where Ava is?

And even though I could get in trouble for sending it, I wrote Lucia's name on it and handed it to Wyatt. Hoping he'd pass it to Lucia. Then I wrote a note to Todd.

I need to talk to you. Alone.

I tossed the note onto his desk, but it bounced onto his shoe. Luckily, he picked it right up and unfolded it. But then I turned around. Because I didn't want him to see me watching him read the note.

A piece of paper landed next to my arm. It was Todd's note.

Cool. Lunch?

I smiled. Todd wanted to spend lunch with me. Just the two of us. Then Lucia's note landed next to me.

She puked four times yesterday.

She puked? Four times? After the mall? I flipped around and glared at Mint. This was the last straw. I could no longer publicly support her even if she was my own flesh and blood. Stealing my real friends' crushes was bad enough, but now she was actually making my real friends ill. This could not continue. I had to stop her. And that meant talking to Todd. Because there was no way I could allow them to remain friends. It had to end. Today. At lunch. And I was prepared to say whatever was necessary to make that happen.

· 22 ·

As Todd and I filed out the door for lunch, he ended up walking next to Kimmie and Jagger and sort of Mint.

"So the premise for the new game is that a zombie virus has struck both the iron and steel dwarf populations," Mint said. "And so the iron and steel dwarves have to unite to fight the new zombie dwarves and prevent dwarf extinction."

"That sounds intense," Todd said.

"How do you kill a zombie dwarf?" Jagger asked.

"Only one way," Mint said. "You've got to sever its head with a magic axe." She drew her finger across her neck and stuck out her tongue.

"Awesome," Jagger said.

What was wrong with these people? Severing heads

with a magic axe was not awesome. As I examined their group dynamic, it became obvious what I needed to do: I couldn't waste any more time. Instead of talking to Todd at lunch, I needed to talk to him right now.

So I reached out and touched him. And when I did this, an electric zap of static traveled through me and onto him. We both got shocked. Hard. Just like at his house.

"Ouch," he said as he kept walking down the hall.

I decided to just ignore that fact that I'd zapped him a second time. "Can we talk before lunch?"

I thought back to the two times we'd touched hands. Had he reached out to me? Or had I reached out to him? The more I thought it over, it seemed like we'd both reached out at the same time. So I kept swinging my hand a little bit closer to his. But he never reached his back out. *What did it mean?* I wasn't totally sure.

"Okay," Todd said. "See ya in the lunch line."

I shook my head. That wouldn't work. I needed to tell him personal things.

"Todd," Kimmie said, interrupting us. "Have you seen Mint's new diagrams that depict the advancing glacier?"

I was so sick of Kimmie. And I didn't remember an advancing glacier in that stupid wolf book. It was like their group was putting anything they wanted into their play as long as it had something to do with a snowy climate. It was pretty lame.

"Yeah, they're great," Todd said.

"The assignment is only worth a hundred points," I

reminded her. "I mean, I really think you're going over-board."

Kimmie's eyes looked big and round and so astonished. "When you're given a resource like Mint, I think it makes sense to go a little overboard."

And then Todd laughed at this. *Laughed.* What was so funny? I honestly didn't see what was funny. I suspected that Todd could tell I was upset. And so he blinked at me in a concerned way with his soft brown eyes. "Let's just talk here. At our lockers."

I nodded. Once everybody left, we'd be alone and I could tell him how I really felt.

"What's up?" Todd asked me, looking around like he was already ready to leave.

But when he asked me those words, I didn't know quite where to start. I didn't want him to think I was just com-plaining about Mint because she'd become extremely pop-ular and I was jealous. That wasn't *really* why I hated her. It was much deeper than that. It was hard to find the right place to begin, so I just said the first thing to come to my mind.

"You look really nice today."

He stared at me. "Thanks."

But then I didn't say anything else. Todd blinked again and waited like he expected me to ask my question. "So what do you want to talk about?"

Wow. Todd was so direct.

"Mint," I said.

"Oh," Todd said. "I think I know what this is about."

"Really?" I asked. I loved the idea that Todd somehow knew what was on my mind before I told him what it was.

"Jagger told me that things didn't exactly work out for her to move here, so she's going back to Alaska in five days," Todd said.

"That's true," I said, because things here had not worked out well for her at all.

"You want to throw Mint a surprise going-away party," Todd said. "Don't you?" Then he reached out and lightly punched my arm. "You love surprises more than anybody I know."

I felt myself shake my head at this. Throwing Mint a party was the last thing I wanted to do.

"Jagger will want to help," Todd went on. "For sure."

"Right," I said slowly.

"I bet it's going to be huge," Todd said. "I mean, we need to invite the whole class. And maybe some of the seventh and eighth graders. Will you invite the other class captains?"

"Um . . . that's a lot of people," I said. "I'll have to check with my mom." *Check with my mom?* What was I doing? I wasn't supposed to be planning a party for Mint. I was supposed to be telling Todd how I really felt about everything.

"Her favorite dessert is Boston cream pie," Todd said.

How does he know that? Does he know my favorite dessert? Staring into his soft brown eyes made my heartbeat speed up. He needed to stop thinking about Mint. He needed to start thinking about us. This was up to me. It was time for me to tell Todd that Mint was actually an evil and manipulative person who didn't care about anybody but herself. I wrung my hands. I put them in my pockets and took them out of my pockets.

"What's wrong?" Todd asked me.

I took a deep breath. "Mint is not who you think she is."

Upon hearing this, Todd's face made three different expressions. First, surprise. Second, suspicion. Third, confusion. He glanced at the glacier sketch Kimmie had given him.

"What do you mean?" he asked.

I thought it was a good sign that he wanted me to elaborate.

"I mean that Mint is a fraud," I explained.

He kept looking at the glacier diagram. "Huh?"

"She wants everybody to think that she's super cool and interesting, but she's actually really weird. I mean, she took a taxi from the airport and she ended up flirting with the cabdriver the whole way to my house."

"Really?" Todd asked. He looked like he didn't believe me.

"Diego," I said. "She's still writing about him in her journal."

"Are you sure?" Todd asked.

"Yeah," I said. "And she's destroyed some of my clothes while she's been here."

"How?" Todd asked.

"She trashes them with paint," I said.

Todd nodded. "Yeah, but they still look cool."

What a rotten thing to say to me. They did not still look cool.

"You shouldn't try to defend her," I said. "She has a very evil other side."

"It's just so hard to believe," Todd said.

What was so hard about believing it? "Well, Mint acts a lot nicer than she actually is."

Then Todd did something terrible. He squinted at me like he doubted what I was telling him. We had such a long history together. How could he doubt me?

"Did Ava tell you to tell me this? Is this about Jagger?" Todd asked.

I was floored. How could Todd even think that?

"Ava threw up four times yesterday and I haven't even talked to her," I said. The words raced out of me. Only after I saw Todd's face flood with disgust did I realize maybe I shouldn't have told him about Ava's vomit issues.

"Gross," Todd said.

That word was tough to hear, because it basically meant that he thought Ava was gross and Mint was cool. That wasn't what I wanted him to think at all. "Forget what I said about Ava throwing up," I said.

"I'll try," Todd said.

I took another deep breath. "Ava didn't send me to talk with you. It's just, I don't know. Ever since Mint showed up, everything has changed."

Todd looked at me as if he wanted me to explain more. So I did.

"Everybody talks about her," I said.

"She's interesting," Todd replied.

Gag.

"Maybe. But stuff changed between us too. I don't see you as much anymore," I said.

"What do you mean?" Todd asked. "I feel like I see you now more than ever. I mean, I get to hang out at your house and make props."

He was missing the bigger picture. "Not with me. You make props with Mint and you also play that dwarf game with her."

"We were assigned to be in the same group," Todd said.

"But she's leaving! She shouldn't have even been assigned to a group. Her grades don't even matter." But I stopped talking before I revealed more.

"Wow," Todd said. "You're really upset."

I was beyond upset. And it was clear to me that I wasn't going to be able to change Todd's mind about Mint. So I moved on to the next thing I wanted to talk about with him.

"So are we going out or what?" I asked.

"What?" Todd asked. "What are you talking about?"

"Don't act like you don't know what I'm talking about," I said. "Are we going out?"

"I asked you if you wanted to go out at the end of summer and you said you didn't want to be official," Todd said.

Regret tumbled through me. I'd just been nervous. That wasn't how I really felt. "I don't think those were my exact words."

"Lunch is going to end. Let's go eat and talk about this later," Todd said.

Things felt very unsettled, but I didn't want to pressure him any more.

"Okay. I need to get my wallet," I said. I'd left my lunch money in my desk.

"I'll save you a place in line," Todd said.

Cool. If he was saving me a place, it meant I hadn't freaked him out.

And that was when I went back into Mr. Guzman's classroom and saw Ava.

"You're feeling better!" I cheered as I raced toward her.

I didn't even realize she was standing at the wrong desk. I didn't realize that until she said, "Shhh. I've got four more desks to go, and I've got to finish before Mr. Guzman comes back."

"Finish what?" I asked.

That was when I saw the notes. They had our classmates' names written on them. Uh-oh. Did Ava write crazy mean notes about Mint to our entire class? That would probably be a mistake, because, as unbelievable as it was, our class really seemed to like Mint.

"You probably shouldn't be doing that," I said as I watched Ava stick a note inside Jagger's desk.

"People need to know," Ava said. "They need to understand what a mean, judgmental dweeb your cousin is."

Complaining to Todd about Mint was one thing, but notifying our entire class in writing seemed extreme.

I saw that the last note Ava put inside somebody's desk had Mint's handwriting on it. The only time I'd ever seen Mint's handwriting was in her diary. Were those notes from her diary?

"What are these from?" I asked.

Had Ava broken into my house when I was at school? That was totally crazy. Was Ava totally crazy?

"Her diary. When I was over at your house for our three-way call, I took pictures of some pages with my phone. I printed out the best sections and voilà! I'm ruining Mint's life."

"Ava! What do they say?" I asked.

I hadn't read Mint's journal, but I sort of thought Ava should describe the contents of the messages right now. I should know what she stuffed in our classmates' desks.

"I used the pages where she says stuff about people in our class and Mr. Guzman and Diego to create a collage!"

I blinked a lot. Like maybe if I did it enough I could blink away reality and turn this all into a dream. Of course, that didn't happen.

"This is a bad idea," I said.

"Maybe," Ava said. "But I didn't ask for Mint to come to Santa Fe and wreck my life. And it's only fair that I wreck hers."

"Let's think this over," I said. Yes, Mint had come to Santa Fe. And somewhere in her inability to blend she'd stolen that light that usually glowed above Ava. But was that light really supposed to glow all the time? Was it possible to share the light? Should you really destroy somebody for just being such a weird and unique person that they wind up on the news and go viral?

And then Mr. Guzman walked into the room.

"Well, it's too late now," Ava said.

"You shouldn't be in here during lunch," Mr. Guzman said.

"I forgot my money," I said.

"Mr. Guzman!" a voice yelled. "The water fountain won't shut off. It's like a monsoon! Come quick!"

Mr. Guzman hurried out. And it was as if I'd been given a gift. I lifted up Todd's desktop and grabbed a note. As quickly as I could, I unfolded it and saw that at the top there was a title: *Here Is What Mint REALLY Thinks of Us.* Then there was a list of quotes in Mint's handwriting. The one with my name in it caught my eye.

Lane should go to clown college. She has an awful sense of humor.

"I have a great sense of humor," I said.

But Ava didn't want to listen to me defend myself against Mint's stolen diary quotes.

"Leave it," she said, grabbing the list from me and shoving it back in Todd's desk.

"Ava," I said. "Give that back to me."

"No." She climbed onto Todd's chair and sat on his desk. "He deserves to know what your awful cousin thinks."

Did he? Did Todd need to know what else Mint wrote

in her diary about him? Did I need to know what else Mint wrote about me? I didn't think so. As much as I hated my cousin right now, it felt as if Ava had crossed a line.

"I don't even recognize you," Ava said.

"I don't recognize *you*," I said.

"Girls. You can't be in here during lunch." Mr. Guzman entered the classroom again and flashed the lights on and off.

And so I walked out of the room.

What did she say about everyone else?

All I knew was that people were going to be hurt and lives were going to be changed. And there was nothing I could do.

• 23 •

My life as I knew it was ending. And so was Mint's. Things began falling apart right after lunch. Tuma approached me. And he looked upset.

"Is it true that *your cousin* is leaving to go back to Alaska?" he asked. His face was pink and pinched with anger.

"Yeah," I said.

"Good!" he said. Then he stomped off to his desk.

He knew. Tuma had read the insult list. I sat at my own desk and held my breath. It was only a matter of minutes. Maybe even seconds. I picked up my Algebra Readiness book and held it close to me.

"Lane," Lucia whispered in a voice way too loud to be a whisper. "Lane."

I didn't know what to do. Why should I have to deal

with any of this? With my Algebra book still in my arms, I jumped up and hurried over to Ms. Fritz.

"I really need to go to the bathroom," I said. Normally, I would have phrased that differently. I would have simply asked for a bathroom pass. But the pressure had gotten to me.

"Let me get you a pass," she said.

But I didn't even wait for one. I just ran out of there.

"Lane!" somebody called behind me. I looked. It was Lucia. But I didn't stop. I sped down the hallway past an open classroom door. Derek waved as I raced by.

"Lane!" Lucia called again.

Her sneakers squeaked as she chased me. Then I heard the sound of another pair of shoes. I turned around. Now I was being chased by Lucia and Derek. I sped up. When I reached a door that led outside, I burst through it. Once daylight hit me, I paused. Because where was I going to go?

"Lane!" Lucia said as she pushed the door open. "Stop."

Derek was there too. All three of us stood outside the building staring at each other.

"Did Mint really write these things?" Lucia asked me, her voice filled with anger.

The bright sunlight continued to pound me. "Um," I said.

"Tell me!" Lucia said.

"Calm down," I said.

"Your friend is really hyper," Derek said.

Why was he even here? I mean, he really did not belong in this picture.

"Derek," I said. "You should go back to class."

"First tell me what's going on," he said. "Is this about the flash mob?"

An hour ago my life had problems, but they were simple. My cousin was in a flash mob and I hated her but she was leaving town soon so it didn't really matter all that much. Now my problems were much more complicated.

"No," I said.

"I really want to talk to you alone," Lucia said.

She was right. "Derek," I said, gently touching his elbow. "This is private."

He seemed a little hurt when I said that. "So you only want my help when you're desperate?" he asked.

He seemed pretty upset, and that surprised me. "I didn't mean it *that* way," I said, trying to sound as kind as possible. "But this isn't about you."

He stiffened and looked even more hurt. "Fine," he said. "Peace out."

And he was gone just like that.

"What was that about?" Lucia asked.

I didn't know how to explain Derek's behavior. And I certainly didn't want to confess that I'd asked him to spy on Mint. So I dodged all her questions. "Lucia, that's like the millionth question you've asked me in the last ten minutes," I said defensively. "I don't know the answer to everything."

"Don't snap at me," Lucia said. "I'm just trying to be a good friend."

Lucia was right. This wasn't her fault, but I wasn't sure how much to tell her. I didn't want to rat on Ava for putting that list in people's desks. And I didn't want to rat on Mint either, even though I couldn't stand her, because it seemed unfair to steal somebody's personal thoughts.

"I'm not exactly sure what's happening," I said.

"Let's forget Derek and focus on the list. It looks like Mint's handwriting," Lucia said. "Who put the list together? Was it Ava? Was it you?"

How could Lucia think I would do such a thing?

"I don't really know what to tell you," I said.

"People are so mad," Lucia said. "Rachel cried."

That sucked. Didn't Ava think about the consequences of making an insult collage? This wasn't just about Mint anymore. "What did the list say about Rachel?" I asked.

Lucia didn't answer me. "The problem with the list is that it's sort of true, but it's stuff that nobody really says. Observationally speaking, whoever wrote these things was very accurate."

"I don't think so," I said. "Mint said I don't have a good sense of humor and need to go to clown school, and that's seriously inaccurate."

"I knew Mint wrote the quotes!" Lucia said.

I couldn't believe Lucia tried to trick me during a time of crisis. "You should show me your sheet," I said. Ava hadn't given me one, and I felt I needed to know what Mint had said about everybody.

"Okay," Lucia said. "But they're mean."

This insult list was just as awful as I thought it would be.

Lucia has a big wart on her hand. It looks worse than Ava's cello callus.

Kimmie took off her socks in the kitchen and her feet looked like potatoes.

Squids have three hearts and are extremely intelligent. I bet a squid could beat Rachel on an IQ test.

Todd was such a follower on the pirate ship today. He is clueless when it comes to strafing.

Felipe's dog and his mom have the same hairstyle.

On Thursday, Mr. Guzman smelled like a pizza fart.

Paulette complains about PE way too much. She is such a weenie.

I find Diego fascinating. Except I wish he didn't have smoker's breath.

Coral Carter is delusional if she thinks Tuma likes her. She needs to enter reality and breathe.

Saw Ms. Knapp at the grocery store buying hemorrhoid cream, superglue, and a piñata. Freaky.

Tuma has slumpy shoulders. He should try doing push-ups.

If Jagger got lost in the woods he'd die, because he has zero sense of direction. It's why he gets stuck in the slime caves forever.

"Okay," I said, thrusting the list back at her. "I've read enough."

"But you didn't make it through the whole thing," Lucia said. "She mentions some people more than once."

"Yeah," I said. "I get it."

I thought what Mint said about us was a little bit mean,

but not nearly as mean as what Ava had done by going through her diary and selecting the quotes.

"How can Mint keep going to school?" Lucia asked.

"She only had two more days," I said. "She flies out on Sunday."

"I don't think she can make it two more days," Lucia said. "Our whole class hates her. Even the nice kids."

This sucked. I thought back to my dad's words on Mint's first day of school. "She's your flesh and blood. Protect her." I pictured her trapped in the classroom like a caged animal. Helpless. And also ridiculous-looking, because today she'd insisted on wearing a shirt she had bought off the Internet emblazoned with the words NORTH DAKOTANS CAN DANCE!

I opened the door to the school. "You go back to class. I've got to get her out of there."

I walked straight to the office and told the secretary that I wasn't feeling well and that I needed to call my mom. And then, when I got my mom on the phone, I told her something that was pretty close to true. "Please come pick up me and Mint right now. We're both sick."

The secretary frowned at me sympathetically, as if she was sorry to learn this.

"Do you want to wait here and I'll go get your cousin?" she asked.

That sounded like a great idea. "Yes," I said, taking a seat in a chair beside her desk. "Angelina Mint Taravel. She's in Ms. Fritz's class."

As I sat there waiting, I wondered what Mint would

say to me. Would she yell? Or maybe she'd give me the silent treatment? Maybe she'd give me a combination of those things. Or maybe she'd realize this was all Ava's doing and not blame me at all. Then I stopped wondering about what Mint would do, because she entered the office and was standing right next to me.

"So I'm really sick, huh?" Mint whispered angrily. "Okay. I'll wait for your mom out front. Why don't you stay and wait right here."

She looked furious. Didn't she understand that I was trying to help her? I felt that I needed to let her know that I really hadn't had anything to do with this mess. Really, we were both victims. But she didn't want to hear it. She turned to leave.

"I didn't do it," I told her.

Mint flipped back around and glared at me. "I know exactly what you did, and I'll never forgive you." She stomped out of the office, fuming like the most furious person I'd ever seen.

So this was how she was going to react. I thought maybe I could fix things by explaining a little bit about how this had happened. "It wasn't me," I called after her.

"You were part of it," Mint called back. "You had to be. And there's no way you can deny that."

Was I part of it? Technically I was not. If you find out about something after it's happened, how can you be considered part of it?

Mint kept walking. Even though it would have been easier to sit in the chair and wait for my mom, I chose to follow my cousin. I didn't want her to hate me. I mean, I understood that she should hate Ava. But I was practically innocent. Also, it was against school policy to leave the building without a parent.

"Stop following me," Mint said.

"We have to wait inside," I said. "School rule."

"This isn't my school anymore," she said. "I don't care." She dropped her backpack on the ground and sat next to it.

"Mint," I said. "Don't overreact." I could only imagine what this day must have felt like for her. First she was sailing the highest of highs from being made famous by a roller-skating flash mob. Then she was slogging through the lowest of lows from having her secret journal full of rude comments distributed to the class. "Please calm down."

"Don't tell me what to do!" Mint said. "As soon as I get to your house, I'm emptying out all my drawers and packing my bag. You can have your stupid room back."

She put her head in her hands and stared at the ground. During her whole stay here, I was so eager to have her gone from my life. But I hadn't wanted it to happen this way.

Before I could coax Mint back inside or the secretary could come out to request that we wait inside, my mother pulled up. Mint leaped to her feet and raced to the car.

"Where's your jacket?" my mom asked me.

That was in my locker along with my backpack and homework and phone. But I did not want to go back inside that building.

"I left it in my locker," I admitted. "With my backpack."

• 245 •

"Do you need it?" she asked.

As much as I didn't want to go back inside that building, I also couldn't imagine not having my phone with me during this time of crisis.

"Wait one minute," I said. "I'll go get it."

Then I raced back into my school as fast as I could and took a turn so fast that I almost skidded into my classroom door. Lucia saw me through the window and jumped up. I hurried to get my things.

"I'm going to check on Lane and give her our Algebra homework," I heard Lucia tell Ms. Fritz. Then she slipped out into the hallway while I was at my locker.

"This just keeps getting bigger," Lucia said.

"Ugh," I said. It seemed like not that much could have happened since I'd been gone.

"Okay. I don't know if you know this, but your mom sent emails inviting everybody to Mint's going-away party at your house. Tuma just got his," Lucia explained.

That made sense. Tuma always snuck his phone into class.

"That party is going to be tense," Lucia said. "*If* people show up."

My mom had asked me if we should invite people from other grades to the party, but I'd sort of blown her off because I didn't want to draft Mint's invitation list. But now I wished I'd played a greater role in it. Who was supposed to be coming to this thing?

"That party is probably going to suck," I said.

"People hate her," Lucia added.

"*I* might not even go to that party," I said. Why should I put myself in such a painful situation?

"Yeah," Lucia answered. "I predict that's going to be a very lonely place."

I took my backpack and raced to the car. When I climbed in, Mint already had her eyes closed.

"Mint says she thinks you got food poisoning," my mom said as she pulled out onto the road.

That was a terrible sickness to try to pretend to have. Because it went away in a few hours. We needed an illness we could fake for the rest of the week. Or maybe our lives.

"Or it could be the flu," I suggested.

Because that was a condition I could try to fake until Mint left town and beyond.

· 24 ·

Mint never told my parents about the list. And neither did I. When Mint relocated to the living room, they assumed that we'd finally reached our limits with each other. Which was sort of true. And while I wouldn't have put it past them to try to drag us to play mini golf together one more time before she left, they used better judgment and did not try to force a friendship-building exercise upon us during our final days together.

I knew that for the next two days school was going to be a world of suck. And I knew Mint knew that too. Everybody in the sixth grade knew that. I was dreading it more than I'd ever dreaded anything. And I was pretty sure Mint was too.

Waiting in silence at the bus stop, she paced in the dirt.

What do you tell somebody who has to face a classroom filled with people she has publicly insulted?

We got on the bus and sat in separate seats. Not that many kids from our class rode this bus, but there were a couple. Tuma plopped down next to me even though he usually sat toward the back.

"Did your cousin write that list?" he asked.

I couldn't believe Tuma was even talking to me. He never talked to me. He was usually too busy skateboarding or talking about skateboarding or texting one of his skateboarding friends. I couldn't believe Tuma even cared about the list.

"I don't know anything," I said.

He knocked his shoulder against me in a forceful way. "You need to practice lying."

Then I watched Tuma walk down the aisle and sit next to Mint. I don't know what he whispered in her ear. I just saw a bunch of head shaking. Then she turned and shoved him. It was shocking. Mint shoved Tuma! And he landed on his butt in the aisle. It was tense. But when Tuma got up, he was laughing. Was Mint laughing? Maybe people would think the list was funny? Mint turned and I caught a glimpse of her face. She wasn't laughing. She looked like she was on the verge of tears. *Everything will be okay,* I told myself. *Two more days of school.* I chose not to think about the going-away party.

As soon as I stepped off the bus, I saw a line of people waiting for me: Leslie Fuentes, Robin Galindo, and Derek.

"We need to speak with you immediately," Robin said.

I walked toward the school just assuming that we'd talk in the meeting room next to the secretary.

"No," Leslie said. "We need to go where nobody can hear us."

I didn't even know the class captains did that.

"Do we need to find Fiona?" I asked.

Leslie snorted. "She's a fifth grader. She can't help us."

"Yeah. We need to discuss sixth-grade issues," Robin said.

"I can't believe you didn't call and warn me about this," Derek said. "Is that what your friend was mad about?"

I couldn't believe that Derek expected me to call him. Why should I have warned him? Was this related to the crush he had on me? Because he wasn't even in my class. As a seventh grader, he was beyond the list. Didn't he know that?

I followed the other class captains all the way to the back of school grounds. I'd assumed we'd stop when we got there, but Leslie slipped through a fence and entered somebody's backyard.

"Do you live here?" I asked.

Leslie glanced at me like that was a very stupid question.

"I live here," Derek said.

Ooh. That was surprising. Derek had a big pool and an enormous and perfectly groomed backyard with a large number of lawn chairs, all built-in outdoor grilling area, and canvas-covered hot tub. I hadn't realized his family was so rich.

"Let's sit," Robin said.

We dragged the lawn chairs into a circle. In the distance, I could hear the warning bell ring.

"Let me just mention that this is off the record," Leslie said. "Anything that happens here will be forgotten once we enter school grounds. Agreed?"

"Agreed," Derek said.

"Agreed," Robin said.

Everybody looked at me. "Agreed?"

I was still trying to wrap my head around the fact that we had meetings off the record next to Derek's big pool when Leslie pulled a piece of paper out of her backpack. It was the insult list. "Did you write these?" she asked, shaking it at me.

I took the paper and looked over the insults. Reading them again, one after the other in Mint's handwriting, made them sound meaner than when I'd read them the first time.

"I didn't write any of these," I said, trying to hand the list back to her.

Robin refused to take it.

"Did you put the list together?" Leslie asked.

"No," I said.

"Do you know who did?" Derek asked.

I was stunned that Derek had asked me such a hard question. I thought he had a crush on me and would try to help me more.

"Maybe," I answered, crossing, then uncrossing my legs.

"Either you know or don't know," Leslie said. Then she turned to Derek and touched his thigh. "Great question."

"Who put it together?" Robin asked.

I didn't answer.

"You have to tell us," Leslie said.

Did I really?

"I think it's just a big misunderstanding," I said.

Leslie read from the list.

The class-captain picture looks totally creepy. I hope somebody puts gum on Robin's face soon.

"We had a gum incident with the class-captain photo last week," Robin said. "It's totally related."

This really surprised me. "Somebody put gum on your picture?"

Derek pointed to himself. "Somebody put gum on my face."

I had no idea people were vandalizing our class-captain photo with gum. But I was pretty sure Mint hadn't done it, even though she did chew gum.

"I think Ava made the list," Derek said.

I tried to keep my face from making a reaction.

"And I think Mint wrote the insults," Leslie said.

I stared blankly at Derek's pool as the late bell rang.

"I can't be too late for class," I explained. "My mom will kill me."

Robin stood up and got really mad at me. "Let's not drag our mothers into this."

I didn't think I was really doing that. "Okay."

Robin continued to yell at me. "This has never happened in the history of Rio Chama Middle School! It's embarrassing that somebody would do something so stupid and mean! And we can't have a class captain who's involved."

I stood up to defend myself. "Well, I'm not involved."

"Prove it!" Robin said. "Tell us who made the list. Tell us who put the list in all the desks."

I looked at Robin, then at Leslie, then at Derek.

"Is it the same person who made the list?" Leslie asked.

"Was it Mint?" Robin asked.

I just didn't know what to do. I didn't want to rat on anybody. And I couldn't believe I was thinking this, but I would much rather have been in my drama-filled classroom than Derek's drama-filled backyard pool area.

"I've got to get to class," I said.

"You've got to tell us!" Leslie said. "If you don't, it's a form of class-captain betrayal."

This was too much yelling. I hated yelling.

"We need to take action," Robin said.

"Whoa," Derek said. "I don't know that we need to do that."

It was about time he came to my defense.

"The sixth graders had a meltdown," Derek said. "If Lane tells us what she knows, we should be cool with that and just move on."

I stood there.

"I don't know. I think we need to take *some* action," Robin said.

"Yeah," Leslie agreed. "Until you tell us who wrote the list and put it in everybody's desks, you're on probation."

"That means you don't participate in any party activities, planning or otherwise," Robin said.

"Yeah," Leslie said. "Your mood isn't officially organic anymore."

I didn't even know class captains could be put on probation. "For how long?"

"Until you tell us what you know," Robin said.

So that basically meant I could be on probation the entire time I was class captain, because I didn't think I would ever tell anybody what I knew.

Leslie and Robin hustled out of the yard and I stood there with Derek.

"I can help you with this," Derek said.

It was too much stress.

"Did Ava put the lists in the desks?" he asked.

I stopped breathing.

"Just say her name if I'm right," he said.

I felt hot.

"Okay. Just nod if it was Ava," he pressed.

That was when I took in a big breath of air, and the smell of chlorine hit me wrong and made me so dizzy my stomach wouldn't stop churning. Then something very regrettable happened. Before I could excuse myself or find a garbage can or move away from the pool, I puked in Derek's backyard.

"Lane!" He stepped back so it wouldn't splatter on his shoes.

"Oh my gosh. I'm so sorry," I said, covering my mouth. That was when I realized that some of my puke actually landed in the pool. I watched as my breakfast cereal floated and broke apart into smaller disgusting clumps.

"Me too," Derek said. "We just had it cleaned."

"I need to go home," I said, feeling as if I was going to cry. This was totally embarrassing. "I need to stop talking about this."

"Okay. But don't you trust me?" Derek asked. "I mean, I spied for you."

Derek needed to stop with the pressure tactics. I wiped my mouth with the back of my hand. "I need to call my mom."

"Yeah," he said, taking a quick examination of the spreading puke spot in his pool. "You do."

· 25 ·

When my mom came to get me at school, I was kind enough and smart enough to suggest that Mint come home with us again.

"I can't believe you're both sick at the same time. Maybe it *is* the flu," my mom said. "And right before the big party."

"You should probably cancel it," Mint said.

I was surprised to hear that. Things must have been pretty rough for her in Mr. Guzman's class that morning.

"Let's not make that decision right now," my mom said. "You've spent a whole month building friendships. It would be a tragedy if you didn't get the chance to say goodbye. Plus, we've already bought the hot dogs."

Little did she know that the tragedy had already happened, and all Mint's "friendships" had gone up in flames. And it was doubtful hot dogs could save them.

And so Mint created a sickbed on the couch and I stayed in my bedroom and we did not talk about school or the list or the possibly canceled party.

But I did attempt some damage control by talking on the phone.

CONVERSATION #1

RACHEL: Ava won't tell me anything.

ME: What do you want to know?

RACHEL: Did Mint really write those things? Are they from her diary?

ME: I don't know. You'll have to ask Mint.

RACHEL: But I don't want to talk to her! She basically called me stupid.

ME: Don't take her comment too harshly. She just thinks squids are super smart.

RACHEL: It's rude to think a squid is smarter than me.

ME: Does that mean you're not coming to the party?

CONVERSATION #2

LUCIA: People are freaking out.

ME: Still?

LUCIA: People are obsessing over whether Ava or Mint wrote the list.

ME: What's Ava saying?

LUCIA: Nothing. Nothing at all. She left early to practice cello.

ME: What about Jagger and Todd?

LUCIA: Mint and Jagger fought before class started. I heard them yelling.

ME: Jagger yelled?

LUCIA: Loudly.

ME: What did he say?

LUCIA: He told Mint that he didn't know she was so judgmental.

ME: What about Todd?

LUCIA: He came over and told Jagger that they were both out of the slime caves and should just get over it.

ME: That's good advice.

LUCIA: Nobody wants to come to her party.

ME: What about you?

LUCIA: Yeah, I'll come. I'm not a hater.

CONVERSATION #3

ME: Todd?

TODD: Are you okay? I heard you threw up in Derek's pool.

ME: Who told you that?

TODD: Derek.

ME: I'm okay.

TODD: How's Mint?

ME: Um. We're not talking that much.

TODD: Because of the list? Did Ava do that? She is so lame.

ME: Are you coming to the party?

TODD: Yeah. With Jagger. I thought that list was funny. Sometimes Mr. Guzman does smell like a pizza fart.

ME: Things are okay between Jagger and Mint?

TODD: Uh, not really. But he's coming to the party.

ME: Good. Hey. Did Derek tell you anything else?

TODD: Not really.

ME: Cool.

ATTEMPTED CONVERSATION #4

AVA'S VOICE MAIL: Hi, this is Ava. I can't come to the phone. If you're calling about the insult collage you found in your desk, I don't have anything to say about it. If you have further questions, ask Mint. She wrote the insults.

After having three conversations and listening to Ava's voice mail, I knew for certain that at least five people would be at Mint's going-away party: Me, Lucia, Todd, Jagger, and Mint. I felt bad that more people weren't coming. But when you write a bunch of insulting things about people and they find out about them, there's not much that can be done.

When it was time for dinner, my mom came into my room with a bowl of soup and some crackers. I thought I might get tired of staying in bed. But I didn't feel like that at all. I found the time alone relaxing.

"You don't have to finish the whole bowl," my mom said, setting it on a TV stand next to my bed.

"Okay," I said.

"Do you mind if we sit and talk?" she asked.

I shook my head and she sat down next to me.

"Is there something you need to tell me?"

I shoved a cracker into my mouth. "I don't think so."

"Mint seems pretty upset," my mom said.

"She got sick and is probably canceling the party," I said. "That's upsetting."

"Yeah," my mom said, reaching up and pressing her hand against my forehead. "I think this might be about Jagger."

My eyes got really big. I couldn't believe I was going to have a conversation with my mom about Jagger and Mint.

"Mrs. Evenson caught them kissing," my mom said.

Holy crap! It was sort of a good thing that I wasn't talking to Ava anymore. Because she would have become completely unglued when I told her this information.

"Wow," I said. "I didn't know that."

"She's twelve. He's twelve," my mom said. "These things happen."

I nodded, but I didn't know if I wanted this conversation to continue.

"Jagger is friends with your friend Todd, right?" my mom asked.

I decided to stop this conversation before it started.

"I am not kissing Todd, if that's what you're worried about."

"Well, I wasn't exactly worried about it, but it does relieve me to hear that," my mom said. I watched her stand up and walk to my doorway.

"Don't be in too much of a hurry to grow up," my mom said. "You're at a wonderful stage in your life."

"Sure," I said. I really wanted my mom to leave. I hated it when she started talking sappy like this.

She left and quietly shut the door. I thought I would have time to read my magazine, but instead Mint came into my room.

"I'm still pretty mad," she said as she walked to my bedside and sat on the floor. "But I don't want to leave hating you. That would be a huge waste of my energy."

I agreed with that. I didn't want Mint to leave hating me either.

"Do you feel bad about what you did?" she asked. "I mean, I know we hadn't become best friends or anything. But don't you feel rotten that you invaded my privacy like that?"

I did feel rotten. But not for those reasons.

"It's awful this has happened. But I never touched your diary," I explained.

Mint frowned. "Then how did it happen?"

"It was that day in my bedroom when Todd held up my underwear," I said.

"Did Ava take pictures of my diary with her phone?" she asked.

I nodded. "But I didn't know about it."

"That's the lowest thing I've ever heard of," she said.

"I know," I said. "But I had no idea what she'd done until after she'd put the lists in people's desks."

"Well, I believe in karma, and one day she'll get hers."

"Ava doesn't keep a journal."

"Maybe I shouldn't either," Mint said.

And I didn't argue with that, because clearly journals were dangerous.

"I notice everything," Mint said. "It's a blessing and a curse. I never meant for anybody to see any of my observations."

"Um, are things okay with you and Jagger?" I asked.

"Oh yeah," Mint said. "I smoothed it out. We have so much in common. I bet we stay friends for years."

I was impressed by how confident she was about this. Things with me and Todd always felt so fragile. "What about you and me?" I asked. "Are things okay between us?"

Mint looked up at the ceiling as she spoke. "I was so excited to come here. I had all these hopes for how it would be. I thought we'd be like sisters, studying together, sharing clothes, going to the movies, shopping at the mall."

"I rarely shop at the mall," I said.

Mint frowned. "Yeah, I learned that." Mint got off the floor and moved closer to my bed. "But you already had this big life. It was pretty obvious that you didn't really want me around."

Mint was making me feel terrible. The truth was,

whether she was normal or not, I never really wanted Mint to fit in. And so I never gave her a chance.

"So I tried to get out there and make my own friends. And I tried to give you your space and stuff."

This month could have been so different. But now it was too late. The time was gone. There was no way to get it back.

"I've never had a cousin come and stay with me," I said. "I probably should have handled it better."

She nodded. "Yeah, that's true."

"I understand if you want to stay mad at me forever," I said.

She shook her head. "I don't want that. I wish there were a way we could leave it that we're friends."

After everything that had happened, how was that possible?

Mint extended her hand like she wanted me to shake it. And I thought that was a very generous gesture considering our month together. So I extended mine. And we shook.

"Friends," she said.

"Friends," I agreed. It was such a relief to feel this way.

"I'm going to go hang out with your mom," she said. "Is that cool?"

I nodded. "It's cool with me."

I think I drifted off for a bit, because the next thing I heard was the sound of Jagger's voice waking me from a light sleep. It was coming from the living room. I crept to my door and opened it. I couldn't believe what I saw.

A bunch of people from my school were there: Lucia, Rachel, Paulette, Kimmie, Jagger, Todd, Felipe, Tuma, Wyatt, Wren, and Bobby. They were all grouped around Mint, chatting and drinking what looked like lemonade. Mint had decided to let the party happen. She was so brave. It felt so weird seeing everybody from my school at my house.

My mom walked out from the kitchen and saw me. "If you're feeling better, why don't you hang out with everyone for a while," she told me, walking over and smoothing my hair back. "Dad's grilling hot dogs outside."

"Okay," I said. But as I watched these people mill around my cousin, it sort of seemed like maybe I should stay in my room. They hadn't come to visit me. They'd come to say good-bye to her. Did Mint want me out there? Or did she want her own space? She'd worked really hard to make these friends. I stood frozen in the doorway. But she'd also worked really hard to make sure we were friends before she left. I decided to risk joining the party. So I walked into the backyard, grabbed a hot dog, and stood next to Todd, because that was where I truly wanted to be.

"It's been a rough week for you," Todd said. "Are you feeling better?"

I took a big bite of hot dog and nodded. "Much."

Then he started laughing. And I think he was laughing at me.

"Why are you laughing?" I asked.

And then he did this awful thing. He pointed at me.

"You're laughing at me?" I asked. I could feel myself blushing.

"You've got mustard on your ear," he said.

How had I done that? I tried to wipe if off with my napkin, but this made Todd laugh harder.

"It was a huge glob," he said. "You smeared it."

"I better go look in a mirror," I said.

But Todd reached out and stopped me from going. "I can get it," he said.

It felt almost magical the way Todd brushed his napkin against my ear and removed the mustard glob. "There. Perfect," he said.

I smiled like a huge dork when he said that.

Finally, things seemed mostly repaired, and sixth grade felt exciting again. But that feeling went away when I saw who was waiting in the hot dog line. Robin, Leslie, Fiona, and Derek!

"Cool," Todd said. "The other class captains are here."

My heartbeat sped up.

I didn't want to tell anybody I was on probation. I took a step closer to Todd and watched as all four of them collected their freshly grilled dogs. I didn't know how to react when Derek spotted me and flashed me the peace sign. So I waved. Then they all started walking toward me. Sixth grade was a total roller coaster.

"Hi, guys," Leslie said.

"Hi," Todd said.

My mind kept trying to figure out the best thing to say under these conditions. But I ended up speechless.

"Can we talk to Lane alone?" Robin asked.

No!

"Sure," Todd said. "I was about to get some chips."

I watched in sadness as Todd abandoned me.

"This week has been totally crazy," Robin said.

"Never in the history of Rio Chama Middle School has so much drama affected so many people," Leslie said.

A cloud darkened the sky overhead and I knew what was coming. They'd decided to get rid of me. They wanted to protect the reputation of the class captains, and that meant cutting me loose.

"Mint called us and explained the situation," Robin said. "And things are cool."

What? "Cool?" Did that word mean what I thought it meant?

"I'm not on probation?" I asked.

"You heard her," Derek said. "Things are cool."

He smiled at me and looked deep into my eyes. Everything was forgiven. Even the pool puking. That was what his smile told me.

"I brought back a bunch of chips," Todd said, passing around a half-full bag.

"Look," Fiona said. "They're *organic* corn chips."

"That doesn't surprise me," Leslie said.

Soon the other class captains drifted off.

And for the rest of the party I stayed in the background. Mint flitted around and talked with everybody. And I mostly talked to Todd. I was a little surprised that people could move past the insult list so quickly, but I guess deep down they really liked Mint. And if they had a choice to be mad at her until she left or forgive her before she left, they wanted to do the latter. Which I thought was cool. Because that was what I wanted too.

· 26 ·

Not everybody forgave Angelina Mint Taravel before she left Santa Fe. But I did. She hugged me at the airport and said, "I hope you come visit me."

My mom overheard her. "We'll try to make that happen this summer."

"It would be great to finally meet Clark," my dad said.

I hesitated. "Is summer really the best time to go? Shouldn't we visit in winter, when the bears are hibernating?"

Mint smiled at me. "You have the best sense of humor." Then she threw her arms around me and squeezed me so tightly that she started to put pressure on my internal organs.

"Thanks," I said.

"I am going to miss this place," she said.

And then I said something that really surprised me. "Yeah. This place is going to miss you."

"I knew it!" Mint said as she entered the security line. "I knew you'd miss me."

Even though that wasn't exactly what I said, I thought I'd be nice and let Mint think it was. And then, watching Mint walk away, I realized that I wasn't just being nice. I really was going to miss her. Not in the same way I would miss a best friend. But I'd miss her the way you miss a cousin who shows up for a little while and shakes up your world.

The farther away Mint got, the more I waved. When I finally stopped, my dad put his arm around me and said, "Don't worry. You'll see each other again."

The whole time Mint had been in Santa Fe she'd driven me nuts, and all I'd wanted was my life back. And now I had it. My life. Except it didn't feel like my life exactly. It felt different. I could feel the tears coming. Why did I want to cry?

We watched as an airline attendant helped Mint pass through the metal detectors. Even though she was on the other side of a glass wall, I could see her perfectly. And finally she saw me.

"I still want to teach you how to lick a glacier!" Mint yelled as she sat on a gray metal bench and retied her shoes.

After all the trouble Ava had caused her, I was glad she still wanted to teach me how to lick a glacier. Even though I really didn't want to do that.

"Sounds good!" I yelled.

Mint broke into a smile and stood up and waved to me one last time. "I'm not even joking," she called to me.

"Neither am I," I said.

And I meant it.

· 27 ·

I had never been so nervous for a sleepover before. Rachel, Lucia, Ava, and me. Just like old times, except Ava and I had barely been speaking. I wanted to change that. I wanted to be friends again.

Rachel arrived first, and she had a plate of cookies for us.

"Yum," I said. "These look great." Actually, they were multicolored and multitextured and looked totally weird.

"Mint gave me the recipe. They have gummy worms in them," Rachel said.

Why would anybody want to eat cookies with gummy worms? But I didn't ask that. "It's cool that you keep in touch," I said. It surprised me that I felt that way. But I did.

"Look at the picture she sent me of her new bookcase," Rachel said.

I took Rachel's phone and looked at the photo. Mint's bookcase was actually a series of shelves that were cut to look like heartbeat lines. They looked super weird and barely practical.

"Her new dad made them for her," Rachel said.

I was relieved that Clark was the kind of new dad who would build Mint heartbeat-line shelves.

Knock. Knock. Knock.

I jumped a little. I was really excited but also nervous to see Ava. Except it wasn't even Ava. It was Lucia. I burst out laughing when she walked through the door, because she wasn't wearing a normal shirt. She was wearing one of Mint's old shirts. It said NORTH DAKOTANS CAN DANCE!

"You are so funny," I said, giving her a hug.

"She dared me to do it," Lucia said.

It did bug me a little bit that Lucia was taking dares from Mint, but I had to admit it was hilarious.

"She gave you a shirt to keep?" Rachel asked.

"She mailed it to me last week when I told her that Mr. Guzman's class felt extremely vanilla without her," Lucia said.

"Has she told you what's going on with her and Jagger?" Rachel asked.

"They still totally like each other," Lucia said. "They're trying to make the long-distance thing work."

That was crazy. There was no way that could last. "Let's not talk about this in front of Ava," I said. I was pretty sure she still had strong feelings for Jagger and his laughing styles.

Lucia and Rachel looked at each other with surprise.

"What?" I asked.

"Haven't you heard?" Lucia asked.

"What?" I asked again.

"Ava is basically going out with Tuma," Rachel said.

"No!" I said. "Tuma from our class?" There had to be a different Tuma.

"Yep," Lucia said. "Turns out his parents have made him take viola lessons since he was five, so he and Ava have that in common."

I could not imagine Tuma playing any instrument except the drums.

"Is she totally over Jagger?" I asked. Lucia talked to Ava a lot more than I did.

"Pretty much," Lucia said. "Mr. Guzman actually asked her if she wanted to switch *Julie of the Wolves* parts and take Mint's spot since she left, and Ava said no."

"She turned down the chance to be in Jagger's group?" I asked. That seemed unbelievable.

"She's over him big-time," Rachel said, nibbling on one of her gummy cookies.

Knock. Knock. Knock.

It was Ava! As soon as I saw her standing on my porch, I was flooded by how much I'd missed her.

"Thanks for coming," I said.

"Thanks for inviting me," she said.

I really hoped she was being sincere.

Ava caught a glimpse of Lucia's joke shirt and winced. I guess it was too soon to start making jokes about Mint.

"Put your stuff down in the living room," I said, leading Ava to an area that was littered with pillows and blankets and several bowls of popcorn. Lucia and Rachel trailed us. But things felt a little awkward.

"Hey, Rachel," Lucia said. "Let's see what kind of ice cream they have in the freezer."

"Good idea," I agreed. "I bet we have at least three kinds. Plus some gelato."

"Gelato!" Rachel cheered.

Rachel and Lucia left Ava and me alone in the living room. We needed to mend things. But neither one of us knew how. Luckily, Ava started.

"I'm not proud of what I did," Ava said. "I really lost my mind."

I nodded. "It's almost blown over."

Ava plopped down next to a pillow and began eating popcorn. I joined her.

"She was so weird," Ava said. "I hated her. I've never hated anybody like that before."

I wasn't sure this was the best way to mend things.

"Most people want to be my friend," Ava said. "Is it snobby for me to think that? Because I think it's true. I think most people want that."

I looked into her eyes. It was true. Most people at our school wanted to be Ava's friend.

"Mint didn't care," Ava said. "In fact, I think she didn't like me from the moment she met me."

What was she talking about? Ava was the one who never gave Mint a chance. So I reminded her of that. "Um, the way I remember it was that you thought she was weird and we needed to ditch her."

Ava tilted her head upward and considered this. "Yeah. I guess that was the way it happened. Maybe I'm more of a snob than I realized."

Would it help or hurt this situation for me to agree with Ava?

"How is she doing?" Ava asked. "Back in Alaska?"

"Really good," I said, smoothing my hair and smiling. "She's actually at a new school and she's made a bunch of friends."

"Does she hate me?" Ava asked.

I didn't know how to answer that. "I think she's over it." Ava nodded. "Good."

We were both quiet. We ate some more popcorn.

"If I could take back what I did, I would," Ava said. "I never feel that way about anything. But I feel that way about this."

This made my heart melt a little. Because I knew I'd probably grown a little bit through the whole Mint experience, but I wasn't sure Ava had. Until now.

"It was a mistake," Ava said. "But you can't undo your mistakes."

It meant a lot to me to hear that Ava wanted to take back what she'd done.

"Are you still going to come to my concert?" Ava asked.

"Yeah," I said. "I've got tickets."

Ava smiled and reached toward my hand. She gave it a squeeze. "I overheard Leslie telling Robin that our school parties are going to have a disco theme. That's awesome. Did you come up with that?"

"Ava!" I said. "I can't confirm anything related to our parties until we announce."

She also said everybody was going dressed as a mood. Ava really was an expert at eavesdropping and snooping.

"Leslie is fierce and Robin is fun and you're organic? How did you end up with that? If I had to pick a mood for you, I'd say you're delightful or playful or organized."

I shrugged. "I can't confirm or deny any of this. But I will say that after researching online, the costume opportunities for organic aren't as bad as you think."

Ava smiled. "I'm dressing up as theatrical."

I smiled back.

"Should we go get Lucia and Rachel before they eat their weight in gelato?"

"Yeah." I smiled.

Awroo! Awroo! Awroo!

"Haven't you changed Todd's ringtone yet?" Ava asked. "We gave him a wolf howl as a joke."

"I know," I said. "But I kind of like it now."

Ava rolled her eyes.

"Hi, Todd," I said.

"I thought I'd check in with your slumber party," he said. "Are you having a good time?"

"We're having a great time!" I said, reaching over and pinching Ava.

"Ouch!" Ava said.

"Sounds like somebody is in pain," Todd said.

"Hi, Todd!" Ava yelled.

"That was Ava," I said.

"Is that going okay?" he asked.

"Yeah," I said.

"I'm going to check on Rachel and Lucia," Ava whispered as she hustled out of the living room.

"Bye, Ava," I said, so that Todd would understand that we were alone now.

"Too bad it's too cold to sleep outside on your trampoline. Jagger and I would totally crash your party again."

"That's sweet," I said. "But you'll have to wait until the warm months."

Todd laughed and I couldn't stop smiling. I loved making Todd laugh.

"What do you think you'll be doing at lunch on Monday?" Todd asked.

His voice sounded really flirty and it made my stomach spin. "Eating," I said.

"With me?" he asked.

"Is that what you want?" I teased.

"When two people are going out, they usually eat lunch together," Todd said.

I was so excited. Todd was finally asking me to go out with him.

"Then we should sit at the same table for sure," I said.

"Cool," Todd said.

And I really agreed.

"Hey, can I ask you a favor?" Todd said. He sounded a little nervous.

"Yes," I said. I had no idea what it could be.

"Since Mint left, we need a person to play the part of Miyax trying to escape the helicopter hunters," he said. "Mr. Guzman said we won't be penalized if we perform with just three people, but we've got all the props and stuff. What do you think?"

What did I think? "Of course I'll be your Miyax," I said.

"Maybe I could come over tomorrow and we could practice," Todd suggested.

"I think you should," I said.

"Then I will," he said.

"You're such a flirt!" I said.

"I only flirt with people I'm going out with," he said.

And those were the sweetest words I had ever heard.

ACKNOWLEDGMENTS

I am indebted to all my cool friends who have joined me in a bunch of life-changing adventures: Kristin Scheel, Joen Madonna, Maria Finn, Nina LaCour, Christopher Benz, Brandi Dougherty, Shelagh Fritz, Ulla Frederiksen, Fred Bueltmann, and Tracy Roberts. Memories of the bears, deep water hydrofit, the mountain lion, mini-cot, burrowing owl, baby goats, Alcatraz gardens, and Sam's cake will remain with me forever. Many thanks to the übertalented Heather Daugherty and Vikki Sheatsley for making my book look überamazing. And many thanks to Sarah Evenson for giving me helpful information about squids and art. And many thanks also to Patrick Wolff for answering all my questions about cellos and cello cases and cello injuries. Thanks to Rachel Belnap for helping to spark my middle school imagination. Of course I am thankful again to my kind, amazing, beautiful, *and* hardworking agent, Sara Crowe. You are a bright light in my life always. Last but not least, I owe unending thanks to my husband, Brian Evenson, who enriches my life every day with his love and encouragement and quesadilla-making abilities.

Andrea Scher

KRISTEN TRACY grew up in a small town in Idaho surrounded by cows. She did not think this was cool. And that's why you won't find any cows in this book. She is the acclaimed author of the middle-grade novels *Camille McPhee Fell Under the Bus, The Reinvention of Bessica Lefter,* and *Bessica Lefter Bites Back,* as well as the young adult novels *Lost It, Crimes of the Sarahs, A Field Guide for Heartbreakers, Sharks & Boys* and *Death of a Kleptomaniac.* She lives with her husband, Brian Evenson, in Rhode Island in a tree-lined, cowless city, where she is very happy. Visit her online at kristentracy.com.